It's Saturday

It's Saturday

Michael Barrett

Carnegie Mellon University Press
2005

Book Design: Sarah Fait
Cover Design: Grinning Moon Productions

Library of Congress Control Number: 2004113741
ISBN: 0-88748-441-7

Printed and Bound in the United States of America

10 9 8 7 6 5 4 3 2 1

So many people helped me in writing this book.
Heartful thanks to family, teachers, and friends,
David Lee, Daneen Wardrop, Scott Lasser,
Rennie Sparks, Amous Maue, Ronald Wallace,
Jesse Lee Kercheval, Deborah Bayer,
Maybelle Hsu, Stephen Dunning, Derek Green,
Bill Cashman, and Robert Cole.
My most special thanks to Andrea Beauchamp.
I could not have done it without her.

Table of Contents

HOME

INSTEAD OF SITTING AROUND the pool with the other conventioneers, wearing plastic cow horn head-sets, mooing, and blowing into empty beer bottles, Jim and Sherry stayed in her room and played cards. They sat on her bed with the door closed, card piles skidding between them. Sherry's fingernails were small. Her hands were pretty, and soft. Jim had felt them touch his face last night.

"Remember the cop?" he said.

"Oh god," she said, coloring up. "Don't remind me." The cop had come out of nowhere, hammered on the window shouting "Move it!" that afternoon while they sat talking, looking into each other's faces at a green light. They'd skipped the presentations on bovine antibiotics that morning and gone into Lynchburg, just to get away.

She shook her head, grinning, and looked through her cards.

"Spades," she said, snapping down an eight on the discard pile without looking at him.

He passed through his hand for a spade. They'd hit it off, all right. This thing they had for each other had come on fast. Over lunch, he mentioned his worry and the nightmares he'd been having about his father, laid out back in Michigan with a triple bypass, and she got out a picture, held it up in the busy restaurant for him to see, a smiling man she said was her father, killed two years ago in a highway accident. The man in the photograph looked as though he were still alive, somewhere. Jim wanted to meet the man. He wanted to tell Sherry her father was a good person, a decent man, though all he could do was look at her and, finally, nod. They'd chewed their food like cardboard and stared at each other, then. After lunch they'd walked. God! How beautiful she was when she walked!

"I felt good, being with you today," he said.

"I love hearing that," she told him.

He squared his cards. "You know what I want to do?"

"What?"

"Anything you say."

She smiled, radiant.

"Want to go for a walk?" he said.

"Yeah." Her eyes were shining. They threw their cards on the bed.

On their way out of the room, he reached around her from behind. She arched into him and they held there. Her head was turned, the side of her face to his mouth. They held that way.

Her eyes were closed. "God," she whispered, "I'm melting." He hugged her from behind, arms strong, and pushed his face into her hair.

"I feel like I'm on drugs," she said, nearly laughing. She turned in his arms to face him and their bodies embraced.

Outside, they walked along the strip the Ramada was located on, passing doughnut stands and restaurants, a shopping center, talking low as the sparse traffic glided into the parking lots or just drove by. The stars were lush in the sky. The night air hung cool in the darkness, the sidewalks and driveways clean from last night's rain. They held hands as they walked.

They crossed a parking lot and walked through a field, to an asphalt-and-woodchips playground, where they climbed to the top of a modernistic wooden playcastle. The platform put them up in the air. Under the furry stars, she pressed into him. He felt her down the length of his body.

"I'm glad I came to this convention," he said. "I'm glad I met you."

She smoothed her hands up his back, then pulled away. He could barely see her face in the dark. Some kids ran by, out in the field, shadows blending into the darkness.

"Jim. I don't know what I'm going to do. I don't want to go back." She laughed.

He pulled her and she came to him.

"I won't cheat on my husband," she whispered.

The orange-and-yellow lights of a semi made a box of color out on the road. He watched it go off down the highway. Who was this husband, this guy who wouldn't give her what she wanted and made her settle for half enough? It didn't matter.

"Okay," he said.

"He helped me build that farm. Oh, Jim, I'm married to a man I don't love."

He loved her. He kissed her. His hands cupped her, and they kissed again. The wooden platform seemed to be undulating beneath his feet. Above him, the stars spread apart.

He would give her whatever she wanted. Then he felt selfish, desiring her with all his heart. It didn't make sense, but why should it. Tomorrow he would be leaving, everybody would. The more he tried to understand what was happening to him now, the more the platform rocked and the stars scattered in the sky.

HE WAS LOST. Route 250 was snaking him away from Virginia, through the Blue Ridge Mountains, towards I-80, the big, bi-coastal road that ran straight through Ohio to Michigan. But Route 250 was taking him away from Sherry; and his sense of destination, the pull of home, was gone from his heart. He kept seeing her face. Feeling her hands. The music in her presence. Her fingertips, pressing near his mouth, the taste of her lips. Her eyes.

The wheels caught embankment and he lurched off the winding road. He jerked the truck back on the pavement, heart pounding.

He followed the roadsigns and arrows, concentrating, pointing the truck where they told him to steer, but the landscape swirled, blurring as he drove through it.

"This is fucking crazy," he said. He hadn't known it would make him feel this way.

Route 250 began to flatten, then fell and rose with shallow dips as he crested the Blue Ridge Mountains. Soon he'd be heading down the other side. The thought scared him. He pulled the truck off the road into a tiny rest area overlooking a horizon of lumpy hills. He parked under a cast-iron sign that said the geologic formations were "scenic." He sat wincing in the truck. He wanted to turn back.

"Take me with you," she'd joked when they kissed good-bye only a few hours ago. Now, sitting in his truck at the top of the Blue Ridge Mountains, it wasn't so funny. He had felt completely next to her last night. Now he was tingling, confused. He remembered her telling him, "Anything's possible."

He started laughing. "This is wild," he said. He eased the truck from its resting spot and headed down the mountain.

It was a long, steady drive back, the highway mundane with its false service areas full of exhausted travelers and sugar-drunk kids, and he felt worse with the distance, the bench seat next to him empty, love songs playing on the radio. He arrived at the farm at midnight, stars clustering the sky, Michigan air ringing out around him.

Inside the farmhouse, the kitchen was warm and smelled stale. The refrigerator hummed. Melody cried and he opened a can of cat food, fingertips shaking, and set it on the floor. He was too tired to eat. In the bedroom he remembered he'd made the bed up before he left—the dark blue sheets his wife had liked and the big white blanket—so that he'd be comfortable when he got home.

But as he lay there, the bed felt empty, emptier than empty—subtractive.

JIM HOOKED THE AUTOMATIC milking machine to Isabelle's udder. He remembered, he milked the cows by hand all through his boyhood; once the milk started flowing white through the clear plastic tube, he looked at his hands. The palms weren't calloused, the backs were veined and tanned. He thanked God for his hands. He hoped they would always work well for him, afraid of the damage he might have done exposing them to temperatures so cold they wouldn't open again for half an hour or cutting them open to the shiny white bone while working on machinery.

She liked his hands, she had said, holding one with both of hers. He turned them over, back and forth. He wanted to hold her with them again. He wanted to touch her, to slide his palms down her, around, inward and then to spread his fingers as they made love.

"Sherry," he said. He had been seeing her all week, saying her name out loud as the image of her seized him again and again. He had imagined them together in bed, snuggling at first, then embracing, grabbing each other like kids, then holding each other with all their hearts as, inside her, he gave the satisfying strokes.

The ground was undulating under his feet again. He sat down.

"Damn," he whispered. "Damn," he said. The cows in the milking barn looked at him with their flat, open faces. They chewed their feed and blinked.

The day his wife had driven off to live with the tanker driver from the co-op, Leighton Kirby, the Dodge had been crammed to the windows with artifacts from their fast three years together. She had smiled from the car before she left. Her last word had been "Okay?"

"Why is it," he asked the cows, "that when stuff like this happens to me, all I can do is tell you guys about it?"

HE WAS IN THE BULL PEN, pitching hay through the open gate, when the old man came shuffling out to the barn. He'd been with Jim five days now, out of the hospital. He was starting to get around.

"Hey," the old man said.

The bull was tied to a beam and the old man went over to him. Jim watched as the bull stood still while the old man checked him, touching his back and nose, looking into his ears and eyes. When he was done he walked over to the pen. Jim wanted him to go sit down, but he leaned against the gate, eyes shiny behind soft folds, proving he could stand. He wanted things back to normal.

"Healthy," the old man said, his scar running out the collar of his shirt and up his neck like a pink flesh zipper.

"Breeding him day after tomorrow," Jim said. "Maybe he knows."

The old man laughed. "Which cow?"

Jim thought of the old man's heart beating inside his chest, all stitched up in there with veins from his legs. He had seen a calf's heart once, in a jar of formaldehyde at the vet's office, looking at first like a gob of angel hair, frowsy with swirling heartworms.

"Elizabeth or Jane," he said. "Whoever's hotter." He pitched a fork of hay out of the stall. The old man kicked it into a mound beside the pen.

"So what else happened at the convention?"

Jim stood the fork on end, tines in the hay, and let his arm hang from the handle. "I got plenty of samples. I had a good time."

"Meet anybody good?"

"Yeah—quite a few. This one woman raises Holsteins in upstate New York, she's got them living twenty years, and they weigh fourteen hundred pounds. They give eight gallons a day."

The old man's eyes widened then narrowed. "Must eat a lot."

"Not really, it's all breeding—they just drink more water, is all. It's amazing. It's just breeding, is what she did."

The old man let out a whistle and shook his head. "Damn cows," he said. "What next." Jim knew he'd be surprised.

A shaft of sunlight fell from the door, through the dust in the air to the ground. "Meet anybody?" the old man said.

Jim thought about it. The old man had been to conventions.

"Yeah, I met somebody. I had a good time. You could say I sort of fell in love."

The old man looked at him. "Sort of fell in love? That's a new one."

Jim smiled. "Well, you know. I met a beautiful woman."

"Why didn't you say something? Who'd you meet?"

"The woman I was telling you about. Her marriage is shot to hell. We hit it off pretty good."

The old man scratched his head and rubbed the back of his neck.

"You're going to get something going with her?"

Jim felt resentful. "Like to."

"She's married?"

"Right now."

"What do you think's going to happen?"

"Well, I'll go out there, or she'll come out here for a while, and we'll figure it from there. You know."

"Ain't gonna work, Jimmy. You know that."

The bastard had a lot of gall, coming out interrupting when he should be inside, lying down. "Why not?" Jim said. "Anything can happen."

"Well, think about it. You're trying to turn a summer camp romance into big thing. You don't know what she wants. She's married."

Jim leaned the pitchfork against the corner of the stall. "I told you that's on the skids. Neither of us knows what we want."

"You're going to get yourself hurt."

They stared at each other. "I doubt it," he said.

"Let me put it this way," the old man said. "What do you think she wants?"

"Somebody who cares about her," Jim said. "Somebody who loves her for the way she is."

"That's what I'm saying. Let her be. You got no call to fool with her now."

HE HAD SENT THREE LETTERS but that night, he called. She answered the phone.

"It's nice to hear from you," she said, "but you better not call here."

"Where can I call?" he asked.

"Better not to," she said.

"I want to see you," he said.

"Yes." She didn't say anything else. The line hissed.

"Why don't you come on out here?" he said.

"There's too much going on, Jim. It's not a good time. I just need space now."

"Okay," he said.

"I'll be sending you a letter."

"Okay," he said. He wanted to say exactly the right thing. He let it come to him. "Take real good care."

He hung up the phone. There was a patch on the kitchen floor where an old stove had been. The old man was sleeping in the spare room. Melody was outside, on top of a fence post, watching birds. Jim sat down in a chair.

The light in the kitchen went tawny then dim as he sat there.

The cows had been in the pasture all afternoon and evening. Jim pulled himself up to standing. It was past their feeding. He went to call them and close them in their stalls in the barn.

Outside, the sun had gone down, a band of browns and purples melting over the horizon like a candle. A steel Michigan wind raced along the ground.

"Girls," he shouted from the open gate. "C'mon home." The cows started toward the barn, dull shapes moving slowly in the field grass.

He leaned on the gatepost and watched as they came lumbering through the sifting light. The ground rocked, and he imagined himself at the door of her farmhouse in New York.

"What are you doing here?" he heard her saying. "I told you not to come. I can't go with you. You shouldn't even be here. Go on, get out."

He saw her push the door closed and felt himself push it open, hard, against her resisting arm, then enter and grab her though she slapped him and fought him away, the two of them struggling, furniture crashing as he picked her up and carried her kicking to the wall, where he pinned her though she fought him and kissed her though she turned her face away until she turned to him, and kissed him back, her arms suddenly around him, her hand finding his and grabbing it.

"I want you," she breathed. "Take me with you."

In Michigan the cows wandered clumsily through their gate.

He looked out over the field, and then he was in her house again, on his knees in front of her, head hanging down.

"What, Jim?" she was saying. "Look at me."

He tilted up his face beneath the tops of her legs.

"I . . ."

"What? You what?"

"Please," he said.

"Please?"

His vision smeared. ". . . just some love."

He swallowed.

She looked down, and kept looking.

"I'm begging."

The last of the cows came, bell tinkling, through the gate. He pulled the gate shut, then heard, somewhere out in the field, Annie's calf mooing. He headed out after it.

That's the difference between us and them, he thought as he walked across the field, that's the difference between her and me. She will remember me, but I will always want.

The calf was calling. God, he thought, don't take her away from me.

When he found the calf he stood with it, rubbing its muzzle before leading it back to the barn. It took his thumb into its mouth and began to suck.

"Stupid," he said, pulling his thumb out. He ran his hands down the calf's back and petted its smooth, not-yet-coarse fur. The wind came up from behind him, blowing from the dusk toward the dark, starry east. It was a strong wind, cold; it would carry the sound far were he to yell "Sherry" with all his might.

THE LAST TIME I SAW MY FATHER

HE WAS STANDING IN THE HALLWAY between our bedrooms, grinning, his boots splayed open, their laces loose and dragging on the carpet. He was clapping his hands. "C'mon, kids!" he was saying. "Everybody get some church clothes too!" Batting fell in tiny clouds from the ripped quilts of his insulated nylon jacket, grease-buffed to a sheen where the material pulled tight over his stomach. He smelled like grease, too. I just hoped he wouldn't move around too much. I knew he'd leave a stain in the carpet that would make Mom suffer.

Janie came into the hallway holding the grocery bag he'd given her. "Where we going, Dad?" She pushed her bangs out of her face. She was still wearing her pajamas.

"No honey," he said. "Get dressed." He turned her around by her shoulders and gave her a little shove back into her room. She stamped her foot.

"Grandpa's!" he said like a magician pulling a rabbit from a hat. He came right up on the balls of his feet.

"Wait a minute." My brother held an oxford shirt over his bag. "Does Mom know about this?"

We all knew Grandpa, and we liked him, but we'd never been to his house. We didn't even know where he lived. We only knew that when he came to visit, he brought us bubble pipes and salt-water taffy and told us stories about animals, stories in which the animals talked. We hadn't him in a long time. He'd become a memory, but a happy one among many not nearly so good. Our mother liked him too.

My father walked into our bedroom and mussed my brother's hair. "Of course she does, Kevvie. You know I wouldn't make any plans without your mother's permission." He put his hand on Kevin's shoulder and stared at him through red-rimmed eyes.

"When did you talk to her?"

"This morning." Whiskers white as a badger's circled my father's mouth. He was wearing a soot-smeared day-glo orange watch cap he'd probably worn changing the transmission in a jeep.

"That was you on the phone?"

In the doorway of our bedroom, Toby, our beagle, bared his tiny teeth. Melting snow dripped from my father's boots. He patted Kevin's shoulder, smiling. "Yep." Kevin smiled back, a little uncertainly. We hadn't seen my father in months. He held his smile like he was having his picture taken.

"You wanted to surprise us?"

"Exactly!" my father said. He clapped his hands. "Now let's fill that bag!" He stomped across our room, opened the closet, fingered through the garments until he found a suit coat—one my mother had been inspired to buy for me after seeing little Ricky on I Love Lucy when I was a kid—and stuffed it into Kevin's sack.

"Hey! That's not mine!" Kevin yanked it out and threw it on the bed. He went to the closet and stuck his hands in the hanging clothes and pushed the pile down the rod. He pulled his fist out dangling his navy blue suit by the hanger hook.

"Good Job Kevin!" my father said. He gave Kevin's hair an extra-vigorous mussing and went into the bathroom. I heard him in there, gutting the medicine cabinet of our combs and toothbrushes and toothpaste tubes.

"What's everybody's favorite toy?" I heard him yell. "Everybody pick a favorite toy to bring!"

I WATCHED KEVIN. He was folding his clothes, placing them in his bag carefully, concentrating as if he were assembling something that would last forever. I didn't say anything. We'd been on plenty of short-notice trips with my father over the years—a few birthdays, one Christmas when he lived in a new house on a lake, a weekend here and there after he moved back to town. He'd even followed our school bus once and taken us off a stop before our home when my mother left town to be with my aunt, who'd rolled her car. But my mother was getting a permanent this morning, and she hadn't told us to expect him. He'd whipped open three brown paper sacks the minute we unlocked the front door, handed one to each of us, and told us to go fill them up with "visiting clothes."

I filled mine with a sweater, a shirt, a clip-on tie, my yo-yo, and a pair of jeans. I put in socks and a pair of underwear. Then I found a coat I liked, a red twill jacket with baseball-shaped patches and team names embroidered on the front, and I put it on. It was too small. I sat on my bed wearing it anyway, watching Kevin.

My father came out of the bathroom, his face pounding red, the ends of our toothbrushes sticking gleefully out of his bulging coat pockets. His knees flexed and he punched the air, low, by his stomach. "Everybody ready to go?" he asked with verve, and I said "Yes."

Downstairs we all went, bags in our arms, my father bringing up the rear in his flapping wet boots. The TV was still going in the living room. A black and white dog crawled across the screen through a room on fire. I noticed the fort Janie and I had been making with couch cushions and a comforter when the doorbell rang.

Toby whined at the door looking up with dark brown eyes, begging not to be left in the house.

"Can Toby come too, Dad?" Janie asked.

"Well sure he can honey." My father swept him off the floor with a roundhouse scoop of his arm.

Toby yelped.

My FATHER SLAPPED THE ROOF of a long, white car.

"How's that for style, kids! A Lincoln Continental!" We stood like figurines in a snow globe, clutching our bags. My father had a different vehicle every time we saw him because he ran a used car lot, and while I might have preferred a Stingray or a convertible some other time, my fingers were frozen magenta from holding my sack in the wind, and I only wanted to get inside.

Chrome and white, the Lincoln looked like our refrigerator, but inside, it was warm as a living room, quiet, with deep velvet seats, everything upholstered and carpeted dark blue. Snow swirled around us as we drove through town, past our schools, in traffic leaving sharp black streaks on the pavement. On the highway snow spun around us, billowing like we were flying through a cloud. Toby ran from window to window, barking as big plows passed whirling their orange light beams, scraping pavement, throwing sand and salt. Barns and fields came at us out of the white then went back into it again. My father started a game of Twenty Questions, and Kevin guessed it: the rearview mirror. Then he wanted to know why were we going to Grandpa's.

My father said, "Well I tell you Kevin, that's a very good question, and the answer to that question is, we are going to Grandpa's, and we are going there, because it's his birthday."

"How old's Grandpa gonna be?" Janie asked.

"Honey, that's another good question. And the answer to that one is, I don't know. He's real old."

I looked past the folds of prickly scalp at the back of my father's neck. He had the bright orange needle laying between the six and the five in 65, and he was keeping it there.

"Where we going?" Kevin said.

My father peeled his eyes off the speedometer needle long enough to give him a look, his eyeballs wet and permeated with veins. "Grandpa's," he said.

"Where's he live?"

"Oh, Live Oak," my father told him.

"Where's Live Oak?"

"Live Oak? That's in Florida."

Kevin smacked the dash. "What's the matter with *you*? We don't want to go to Florida!"

"Kevin," my father said. "We're going to Florida to see Grandpa. What would he think if he heard you say that?"

"To hell with Grandpa," Kevin said. He was staring across the seat, mad as a wet cat. "Turn around."

"Kevin, I ought to throw you out right here. You can hitchhike home if you don't wan to come with us. Your grandfather loves you. You think about that. What's the matter with you?"

Kevin reached into his sack and pulled out a copy of *Captains Courageous*. He sat hunched over it, studying it like he was trying to memorize every word. I knew he was mad because he was supposed to play his clarinet in church the next day, and I felt sorry for him. I knew how it felt. The central, inevitable experience of my childhood had been his eclipsing me any time my spirits rose and I did anything good myself, and he'd been outperforming me so long, I'd long since passed the point of even trying anymore.

I dug my yo-yo out of my sack and squeezed it. It was a clear blue Duncan Imperial I had paid for with weeks of saved allowance, and I was getting good with it. I put the dirty loop of string on my finger and let it drop, but it hit the floor, and I couldn't jerk it back up. There wasn't enough room in the back seat.

I wound it up and just held it a while. Then I put it back in the bag. I played Barbies with Janie. She was Barbie, I was Midge. We walked our dolls across the hills of Toby's back. We rode horses and had tea and cookies as he slept between us on the seat. After a while he woke and hung his paws over the edge of the seat cushion, panting.

My father drove us into the afternoon, past fields that went off far and flat, dusted with snow like powdered sugar. There was a feeling of being held and hummed to in the car. I looked out the window, lulled by the ride, and in my tiredness, grass poking through the snow in the fields looked bright green.

I remembered the last morning he lived in our house. My mother was wearing a dress as blue as the sky. She was going around the table, placing eggs onto our plates from a big cast iron skillet. He was dressed for work in a clean white short-sleeved shirt, pungent body odor radiating from his armpits.

"That dress looks like a giant snort rag," he'd said. He had a flat top haircut. He looked at my brother and sister and me, grinning. The hair rose straight off his scalp.

She continued around the table, I remembered, her face mottled, eyes down. He squinted at me, aiming his finger, like a gun. When he winked, his thumb came down, and I laughed. That's when she looked up at me, almost through me, stood there with the skillet hanging from her hand. She went into the kitchen, scraped it over a plate, and sank it in the soapy water.

Outside the car, the air hazed and the sun came out of some hole above us, brightening the road and fields, the horizon sky dark as lead.

It was robin's egg blue, sleeveless with a big belt that went around her waist, closed at a pearl buckle. She was going somewhere that morning She was wearing lipstick. Her mouth was red as a tulip.

With a chop of his fork, my father halved an egg, sucked it into his mouth, and spit it on the plate. Janie was two. She looked around the table at us, picked up the egg from her plate, held it dangling by the edge, and pushed her finger through the yolk. Yellow ran down.

My father's forearms rested on the table top. "Ugh, dear," he said. "This is inedible. I'll have to go to Malnight's now and buy something to eat."

He stood and looked at us kids. "I love you guys." He strode across the dining room, through the kitchen, and opened the screen door. I remembered his back, filling up doorway. He was standing on the stoop, holding the screen open with the toe of his workboot. He laced his fingers and turned his palms out. "Oh well," he said. His knuckles cracked. "Good bye." He did a little two-step out of the way of the door, but before it could slap shut, my mother pulled the skillet from the sink and sprang across the kitchen with it, swinging it over her shoulder like an axe, into the back of his head.

I gripped the car door's armrest remembering the bell I heard as my father's arms shot out, his body collapsing, off the stoop, into the bushes. Me running out there, the last time we were a family. Him in a heap next to the house like a discarded marionette.

WE COASTED BESIDE AN UNDULATING, criss-crossed fence surrounding a horse farm. My father swatted the wheel. "If you need to take a leak, this is the place to do it." We rolled to a gravel-crunching stop. He threw it into park, got out of the car, and dropped into the ditch.

Toby jumped over the seatback and out his door. Kevin got out and disappeared. But Janie and I stayed in the car. I had that feeling of waking up but not being able to get out of bed. I looked at a white, arch-roofed barn with X's crossing its doors, a toy on a hill far away. Horses were galloping in the field, a fuzzy gray one chasing a shiny brown one, back behind the barn, then out they came again, the brown one chasing the gray. "Hey look, Janie," I said. "Horses."

Damp air filled the car.

"We're going to visit Grandpa," she said.

The trunk popped then slammed shut and my father came around with two shopping sacks he spilled onto the front seat: a jar of French's, sacks of hamburger buns, cans of aerosol cheese, plastic packs of salami and bologna, a bag of black licorice bites, Fritos, Doritos, grape jam, a box of Three Musketeers bars, red licorice bites, Cheetos, and an orange. "Look what I got," he said pulling a twelve-pack of Hires from a bag. I went down in the ditch.

The air was cold but not freezing. It was clear and easy to breathe. I felt free, standing among the McDonald's cups and beer cans in the recess by the side of the road. The transmission dropped into drive. "Hurry," I heard him yell. I climbed the berm, lighter, and when I got in, he floored it. We took off sailing, the big car cutting through air, carrying the five of us south.

We spread mustard with our fingers, making sandwiches as we rode. The air parted and solidified behind us, you could feel it. Ice crystals in our root beers melted as we drank them down. Janie made Toby a sandwich, and after he pulled the meat from it and whined for more, she fed him licorice bites until he changed his mind, got down, and ate the bun off the floor. We rode eating candy bars or corn chips whenever we pleased, as much as we wanted, until we couldn't stand to eat any more. Toby stood with his paws on the windowsill, looking out. After a while, he groaned, got down, and curled up on the seat.

That afternoon Janie peed her pants and I helped her change. Kevin read *Captains Courageous* until, finally, he acted refreshed and asked my father to teach him to drive. But my father's hands wouldn't let go of the wheel, and he smiled, saying sorry, we don't have enough time. Kevin read *Captains Courageous* until daylight faded, and then he just looked out the windows, like Janie and me.

We drove by rivers, over big steel brides, on roads high above valleys filled with hundreds of houses, whole towns, their windows tinted yellow like lanterns in the dusk. Then the sun disappeared in a pool of blood, and the darkness came down solid, and it was night when my father stopped again for gas at a little two-pump station. He called Toby out and said to stay in the car.

You could see under the fluorescent lights, everything we had with us scattered everywhere—pop cans, wrappers, clothes, crushed chips, everything mixed together, sticky and warm. He came out of the station and backed up the car beside a vending machine and bought ten Seven-Ups, tossing them onto the front seat as they slapped into the tray. We were next to the bathroom. He said Use It.

"GET UP," MY FATHER WAS SAYING. He was clapping his hands. "Get your church clothes on." Toby lay in a nest of Janie's clothes on the floor looking up at me, his eyes shining in the dark. I was alone in the back seat, and I was scared. Janie was gone. Then I realized she was beneath me, pressed into the cushion, sound asleep. I was lying right on top of her.

He was standing outside the car in his underwear. I couldn't see his face, but he had a bolo tie in his hand, and he was putting on a cowboy shirt. We were on a dirt road, headlights shooting white shafts into the muzzy air. An amethyst band stretched along the horizon, pushing a strip of tan above it. From the dark, beyond the reach of the headlights, came a rushing sound.

I found my clothes tangled on the floor and got out. Straight above, a few stars remained. We were in a graveyard. The motor hissed, idling. Palm trees leaned over our heads, their black fronds combing the air as we changed on a lawn of stones and crosses. The night smelled like a greenhouse. It lay against my skin, damp and warm. When I licked my lips, I tasted salt.

"Get in," he said and we did. My father lowered his window and the tangy fresh air poured in. We passed houses, dull pink, pale green, aqua in the dark; distance hid the faces of large buildings, damp gravel lots flanking their shapes in the straining sunrise. I sat up straight in the back, buttoned my buttons and clipped on my tie as we drove. A Sunoco went by, some billboards, then streetlamps hanging over the road, their bulbs marring the air as we drove beneath them. Traffic signals flashed. Then we were in the city. My body pressed the door as my father wheeled into a parking lot. He veered into a space and jammed it into park. The Lincoln bucked. "Okay," he said. "Get out. Stay with me. You kids follow me."

"Where?" Janie asked. She had her dress on.

My father gripped the steering wheel. He looked straight ahead.

"We're going to see Grandpa now, honey." An arm of her Barbie stuck out from the seat cushions. I grabbed it. "Here," I said and gave her the doll.

Sun sparkled off the pavement as we followed him across the lot, to a hospital. A jumble of ambulances clogged the entrance, one with lights still turning. Red crosses glowed from illuminated signs on white poles everywhere. I grabbed Janie's hand. A set of tall glass doors fell open before us, and inside, the ceiling rose like vaulting over the Wizard of Oz. A huge cross with Jesus hanging off it leaned from the wall above an enormous circular counter. The room was quiet as a library. I smelled sheets. Almost whispering, my father talked to a nurse wearing black glasses, glasses with corners swept into points. She studied a clipboard. "When?" I heard him say.

He looked at us and smiled.

"Yesterday," she said and they continued talking in the quiet, plaintive way of adults. She turned a phone around and he leaned over it, punching numbers.

We went over to the drinking fountain to take turns gulping water while he talked. "Son of a bitch," Kevin said. He wiped sleeve on his mouth. "Some party. He isn't even here." He yanked off his tie and hooked his shirt collar open.

"Where's Grandpa?" Janie asked. I wanted to comfort her, but I didn't know what to say.

"Probably in some nursing home we'll have to go to visit now," Kevin said.

I wasn't so sure, but I didn't want to think about. "He could be," I said, relief lifting me into the free zone as, considering the possibility, I said the words. My father came across the lobby and grabbed Janie's hand.

"C'mon guys," he said. "Let's go do something fun for a while." He led us around the tables and chairs, past plants and rumpled magazines across the carpet, back outside to the lot.

"Where's Grandpa?" Janie asked. My father stopped out in the middle of the asphalt and we stood there. His face looked like a plate. The light of day had come upon the world and was gleaming the pavement as if it were a sheet of gold. It was warm out, and I could feel it getting hot. I could tell it was going to hit ninety.

"Well, honey pie," he said. My sister's chin started wobbling. My father squatted down next to her. "It's okay," he said. "We can visit Grandpa later on. I want us to go have ourselves a big old fine time right now."

"Told ya," Kevin whispered.

"TERRIFIC! THAT'S EXCELLENT!" my father yelled. Kevin waved from a orange safety buoy bobbing far out in the swimming area. Behind him, the ocean went off into blue forever. He had been showing us how well he could do the crawl.

My father sat on a tarpaulin he had taken from the trunk and spread in the sand for a blanket, his face gaping with exhaustion. A cloud of seagulls flew up where Toby ran through them on the beach. My father fell backward onto the tarp with his eyes closed.

His body seemed comical lying there, white as dough, his head sticking off it like the end of a rope, his arms and legs flung out sinewy from his big round belly. His mouth hung open, and I heard him breathing, a sound from the bottom of a pipe. Then Kevin came running up, dripping salt water. "Want to see me do the backstroke?"

"That's okay, Kevin," my father said with his eyes closed.

"Is that a yes?"

"Yes," said my father.

"Then watch."

My father leaned up on a trembling elbow. Kevin ran to the beach and leaped into the water. My father's eyes closed. He sat there propped up, mouth open in its geriatric gape, then fell back on the tarp. The cuff of his boxer shorts lifted, puffed open by the breeze. I saw his cock in there, hanging like a bird from its red-brown, hairy nest.

He had given us each a pair to swim in. "Just like a bathing suit without a string," he explained, pulling them wadded from a box of hubcaps in the trunk. Janie didn't mind. She wore a t-shirt with hers. She was scooping sand down by shore. But my pair felt funny—baggy, patterned with red and yellow diamonds.

Shore sounds—waves, calling kids, seagulls—went up absorbed into the heat. He mumbled something, then said it again: "Why aren't you swimming?"

I didn't know the answer. It hadn't occurred to me even to wonder. I just told him, "I can't."

"Go play in the sand."

I stood up.

"Wait," I heard him say. He sat up, leaning on his arms. "Can you tread water?"

I shrugged. I was scared of oceans, lakes, the deep ends of pools. Whatever this meant, I hadn't done it. I liked the sound of the expression, though. He pushed his body up and walked over the hot beach toward the water. I followed, out onto a low pier alongside the swimming area. He grabbed my wrists and swung me over the brine. When he lowered me in, I started dogpaddling immediately.

"No," he said. He sat on the edge. "Kick like this." He tipped back, cranking his feet in the air. "Swing your arms back and forth." He opened his arms wide and swept them, the angel-wing pattern. "Change the angle of your hands. On top of the water." His hands carved arcs. He showed me the rhythm.

He held me by my hair. He lifted my chin above the swells, held me tethered as I did the moves—and when he let me go, I was treading water. "There you go," he said. I felt like a hummingbird flying. The harmony of my arms and legs flexing together kept me afloat. "Take it easy. You can do it as long as you want," he said, and I knew I could. It was exhilarating! I could survive the Titanic if I had to. I would never drown!

"Way to go." He watched, head drooping. I hovered next to him, looking back. "Take it easy," he was saying. "Breathe easy. You can do it without getting tired." His wrist came to his face. "Do it three minutes. I'll time you." His eyes closed. "Go."

My hands came in. Kevin had a merit badge in lifesaving, a round embroidered thread-picture of a red-and-white life ring with tan rope handles my mother had sewn on a banner he wore with his Boy Scout uniform. The banner was covered with patches. I didn't know what most of them meant, but I felt essentially erased every time he wore the thing. I was dogpaddling, my hands splashing the water. He opened his eyes.

"Swing your arms out," he said. "Take it easy." He checked his watch. "Two minutes."

I spread my arms out but the rhythm was gone. I was flutter-kicking, trying to speed up time. "I can't do it," I said and took in water. He kept his eyes on me. My arms weren't making their sweep. I kicked harder, my hands came in, and I dogpaddled with my head tipped back, coughing. He was studying his watch. "Come on, two more minutes."

"Can't, Dad." My face sank. "Help."

I was going to drown. He looked down at me. I reached up and my face sank but he didn't reach for me. I kicked to the surface. He kept watching. "You can do it," he said. I inhaled burning water. "Keep going."

I was bobbing, my vision of him distorting, flooding green, then coming back silhouetted in blue sky. "One minute."

He leaned over and draped out his arm. I seized it and held it clinging. He hauled me onto the pier and laid me out on the boards. I pressed myself to them gasping. They felt soft and warm, and when I spotted Kevin out by the buoy, I took a full breath and kept breathing. He hadn't seen me.

What my father said as we walked back to the tarpaulin, was nothing. The sand squeaked under my feet. We sat down facing the beach.

The tarpaulin exuded its tar-smell into the superheated air. Toby bayed somewhere in the crowd. He was hollering, running wild all over the beach. I spotted his white tail in the air and his brown, black, and white patches by a lady lying on a towel. He was sniffing the lady's stomach. He lifted his leg and peed on it. She did a sit-up.

"Oh, no," my father said, his voice like a nail pried from wood. He lifted himself from the tarpaulin and hobbled onto the beach, chasing Toby down. He got over him, snagged his collar, and yanked him off the sand. He carried him over to the lady and said something to her. Then he carried him up the dune to the parking lot. I was listening to the distant sounds—lost shouts, squealing kids—when he came back. "He can stay in the car if he won't behave." He crawled to the center of the tarp and collapsed.

"Dad," I said. "Did I make it?" He lay there sprawled out limp. He seemed to be unconscious. He shook his head, slightly: No.

I ate some Fritos and opened a 7-Up, but the Fritos crunched sand and the 7-Up was hot and fuzzed up my nose. I poured it out.

"Sometimes I feel like I'm never going to be good at anything," I said, but to no one, really.

Dune grass shimmered in the breeze, kids played in the water. "It's too bad," he said. "There's nothing I can do about it. Try not to think about it," he said. "It only gets worse." He rolled onto his side and drawing up his knees, grunted, bringing his elbows down and together in a kind of fetal position. "Go play in the sand."

I got up and went looking for Janie. I found her on the shore. She had a hole in the sand she was filling with feathers, bottle caps, shark eggs, and shells. I helped her hunt for more. We gathered them, but the more we found, the more they made me feel like flotsam myself, and I couldn't shake the feeling that somehow, my own life was just another piece of trash. Then I found a piece of driftwood that looked like some kind of animal, silver, and as we kept searching, I began to feel better. I felt good after a while, letting my life take its own course. We searched everywhere. We collected many objects. We played for a long, hard time.

We were popping seaweed pods in the warm shallow water when my father came up marching. "Come on come on come on," he was saying. "Oh, come on. They got an hour's difference here!" He ran to the tarpaulin and spun it in a ball, spiraling sand. "Lordy lord God," he said, fish-belly white on his right side, tan down the middle, his left side sunburned slap pink. "We gotta go."

"Where," said Janie. "Where we gotta go?"

He looked down at her with eyes that were slits. "Grandpa!" he barked.

We found Kevin and climbed the dunes to the parking lot. Our bodies ached as we trudged to the car. We all had sunburns, red against the asphalt. When we got there and unlocked the doors, the Lincoln looked like a cave. Upholstery fabric hung down in long ripped triangles from the ceiling. Toby had gnawed the armrests down to their brackets and was gone, twisted through one of the Lincoln's vent windows. "Put your church clothes on," my father said. He pulled his cowboy shirt from the front seat and started dragging it on. It split somewhere, but he went on dressing. He buttoned it up as if it were brand new.

"Where's Toby?" Janie asked.

"He climbed out the window, honey. Toby went for a walk. Put your dress on." He got it out of the back seat and pushed it over her head backwards.

"Here," I said and straightened it around. We dressed as fast as we could, dizzy in the heat, and got in.

"We're leaving him behind," Janie shrieked as the car picked up speed and we pulled out of the lot.

"No we're not, honey." My father ran up all the windows at once and turned on the air conditioning. "We'll come back for him. Be a big girl now."

She looked out over the seatback through the rear window, sniffling. I told her Toby had our phone number on his collar and that somebody would bring him back. I knew we'd never see him again, but I didn't want her to start crying. Eventually she turned around. We pulled a piece of weather stripping he'd torn from the door jamb between us for a while, and then I just sat back in the coolness, watching the palm trees and buildings in the sun.

"Who can tell a story about Grandpa," my father said. "Who remembers something nice about him?" We were slaloming through traffic. "When I was a kid he caught a baby raccoon and we raised it. We named him Joey. Somebody else say something."

"It's Grandpa's birthday," Janie said.

My father leaned forward in his seat. He wasn't speeding, but he wouldn't slow down. I said, "One time Grandpa took us ice skating and he skated backwards, pulling me and Kevin with his hands."

"Yeah and after that we went to this lady's house where they were making candy canes," Kevin said.

"I didn't know that," my father said.

"There was a bunch of kids there. This lady and her husband, in their kitchen. They poured it on a big table until it cooled. We all got to make our own. Grandpa helped us twist the colors."

I remembered the event, though as having happened another time altogether. They'd come out rock solid, red and white. Mine lasted for days.

"Candy canes," Janie said.

MY UNCLE TONY GLOWERED, handsome in his black pastor's uniform with the white square at the throat. He looked like he was going to spit. "For the love of God," he said. "Hell, Chet."

"God damn it," my father said, his eyes black dots. "He loved them. Is that okay with you? I wanted them to see him. Don't tell me what to do." I thought he was going to slug my uncle in the mouth. Uncle Tony shook his head and turned and walked to where a few people were standing around a mound of copper-colored dirt. We had gotten there too late for whatever else had happened. That, and some flowers, was it. Kevin sat in his suit coat in the car reading *Captains Courageous.* I took Janie to the tombstone and read it for her. It was shiny gray marble with white letters carved into it. Letters on other stones were darker, these were fresh and new. You could almost smell the dust. I subtracted the dates. He was eighty-six.

My uncle Tony came up to us while we were standing there and asked me how my music was coming along, and I told him that was Kevin, so he asked me if I'd been doing much fishing lately, I have no idea why.

I just said no.

I was looking at the pile of dirt my grandfather was under.

It was only dirt, but it didn't make sense anymore. Finally I remembered him showing me a cat's cradle with a piece of string, lacing it on my fingers until I could do it myself, teaching me, and I realized that even though I never knew him very well, he had treated me good. I loved him.

My father drove us away from that place in his long white car. We stopped that night at a Holiday Inn in South Carolina, where he bought us steak dinners in a restaurant called the Clipper Ship, its rich red walls hung with nets and swordfish and steering wheels from ships. We drank kiddie cocktails with cherries and pink umbrellas and plastic swords in them, then we walked past the colored neon Holiday Inn sign to our room. My father took one of the big double beds and lay there, all his excitement gone.

Kevin, Janie, and I shared the other bed, but we couldn't fall asleep. Our sunburns hurt too much. We were too tired even to speak. A sound of ripping air, the highway, came from far off, gushing through the screen. We lay without moving in the dry, warm room. There was that empty brightness of a place where you are lying awake in the dark and can hear your own breathing, the blood pumping in your veins, the pounding of your heart. "We're going home," Janie whispered.

THE NEXT AFTERNOON, somewhere in Indiana, we got lost. Flurries had started in Ohio, fat flakes squalling on gray ground, and the snow kept falling harder the farther north we drove. By the time we hit Indiana it was slanting into drifts. My father had taken a chance, gone searching the Indiana back roads for a shortcut to the highway. Every turn he took put us on a more rural, snowier road. "Weather's always worse the closer you get to home," he told us, but we were going one direction after another. He was taking every turn that came out of the snow. We ended up on a tractor path between two fields, trapped in glacial drifts spreading across a horizonless expanse of white.

He was going to have to back up a long, long way. But where we'd come from was just as lost, and it seemed like there was nowhere left to go. We just sat there.

"We'll be all right," my father said. He backed us out, a long, slow reverse past trees and mailboxes and houses in the storm. He got us on the highway and we drove through whiteout the rest of the afternoon, our pace slowing, past jack-knifed trailers, the rear ends of cars stuck up from ditches, all the way home. We were lucky to have made it. The odds had been against us. The sky had gone dark by the time we crept through town.

The storm had driven the city deserted. Stoplights swung from their cables as we drove, four-foot snow banks on the sides of the streets. Snow was falling through the halos of the lights in the parking lots, lots already full, still filling, snow frantically trying to cover up snow. Our street was gone, a channel where its center used to be.

"Cool," said Kevin. My father drove with his fingertips on the wheel. We rode slowly down our dark street. I could see our house, on the corner of the block. The lights were on.

My father pulled up and put the Lincoln into park. The transmission went though its familiar, obedient routine, clunking into patient waiting mode, engine idling after its thousands of miles. Kevin unlocked his door. "Put your church clothes on," my father said.

"Oh no," said Kevin. "I'm going inside." My father turned on the dome light. "Please," he said. He faced forward. "Show some respect. Look nice for your mother." The house lights glowed, an orange warmth oozing from the windows. I imagined her in there.

Kevin sighed and leaned forward. He dug through his bag.

"That's good," said my father. "You're a good son, Kevin." He reached over and mussed Kevin's hair.

Kevin pulled out his suit coat and put it on. "I can't believe how much trouble you're in."

My father turned around and reached to the floor, groping, brought up Janie's dress by the hem, and tossed it on the seat between us. His face was a mass of creases.

"You can't divorce your grandpa," he said. He reached back and started pulling off Janie's shirt. "Put your dress on." Janie started to cry. She was sunburned. She was red as a valentine. She was crying, sobbing from somewhere deep inside.

Kevin sat waiting with his jacket on. The windows were black outside.

"She can't," I said. "Take your Barbie," I told her. "She's got a dress on."

"Okay," he said. He turned off the dome light and looked down the street. I saw the silhouette of his knuckles on the steering wheel, perched there like the feet of a bird. "I love you guys."

Snow swirled into the car when Kevin and Janie got out, but I sat there. The door was open. I had the feeling that once I got out and shut it my father would drive away and I would never see him again. I was trying to figure something out. There was something I wanted to tell him, but I couldn't even say good bye.

CADILLAC

AFTER MY PARENTS' HOUSE BURNED DOWN, I took the train to see them, in Cadillac. Eating peanuts and drinking Old Fashioneds, I watched the landscape go by. Evansville had been mild and sunny when I left, but snow had started in South Bend, and now in Cadillac there was blowing and snow catching on the ground.

Michigan weather is cold this time of year, I knew that, yet I was only wearing my Levi's jacket. The air was like metal when I got off the train. People met each other on the platform where the snow was sticking, then walked off together, talking. I waited for somebody to meet me. Then I noticed Aunt Rose, grinning and waving to me from her Cutlass.

"Bob and Margie are home," she said in the car, bundled in her coat with a tan bathrobe underneath. "They're so tired." We pulled out of the lot in the swarm of other leaving cars. "Where's Trina?" she said.

Trina was in Evansville and had stayed there on purpose but that's not what I said. "She couldn't get away from the hospital," I said. "She's sorry she couldn't make it."

The truth is, Trina was home with the day off and she was glad about it. Years ago, while smiling and waving to my parents as they pulled out at the end of their first visit, she told me, "Your mother's a bitch, Calvin. Do you hear? A certified bitch." This was because over dinner my mother had said that having a baby without being married was "dirty," by which she meant Tracy, Trina's daughter. It was a harsh thing to say, and Trina was entitled to her anger, I accept that. But though we talked about it, I was never able to smooth things out after that, and we didn't discuss it anymore.

Still, I was mad that she wouldn't come. My parents were too old for that now. Besides, their house had burned down, for Christsakes. They raised me there. You would think she would have some compassion.

But no, she wasn't even working. She was probably watching General Hospital and having a beer.

Rose, who is short, leaned forward to look over the dashboard. I hunched over too, cold, my hands jammed between my legs to get the feeling back in my fingers, even though the Cutlass was warm inside.

"Well it's too bad she couldn't make it," Rose said, craning her neck, driving into the snowflakes. I wiped my window. Outside, the high school went by with its huge new addition. A big Maroon Hornet with shark's teeth was painted on its side, "Get 'Em Hornets!" coming from the mouth. The parking lot, which had been a field of wild strawberries when I went to school there, was filled with cars clotting snow.

The Dairy Boy went by, all boarded up.

"They were lucky to get out, Calvin. Everything's gone."

My father had told me on the phone that the flames went higher than the trees.

"They don't even know what caused it," she said.

"Maybe the insurance company will find out."

"They were there the next day."

"And don't they know what happened?"

"They came over twice and asked questions. So did the police."

"They think they started it."

"I don't know."

I was cold. I wanted a drink. I leaned over and pulled my jacket closed tighter. "Thank God they're alive," I said.

"The police took them to the hospital. But they were okay. I picked them up in the morning. They were so . . . excited."

"They were lucky."

"Everything's gone, Calvin."

I put my hands to the angle of the dashboard in the heat blowing from the defrosters. Rose was driving too slowly, fairly creeping. I wanted to lean over and press her leg on the accelerator pedal. The roads weren't that bad.

"Well," I said, "with the insurance, maybe they can get a nice place, now. At least they have that."

"They don't want to find a new place yet," Rose said, tipping her head, looking over the tops of her glasses at me.

Maybe they didn't. I could imagine their tired faces.

"Well," I said, "it's not fair." Then I said, "It'll take time."

Then I asked if Wayne was coming.

Wayne is my brother, an otorhinolaryngologist in Cincinatti. As long as I can remember, he wanted to be a doctor, which always suited my parents.

"Wayne couldn't get away from his hospital, either," Rose said.

He was probably at a convention or in the operating room, practicing microsurgery techniques. So he had an excuse not to be in Cadillac, unlike Trina. Back in Evansville, I figured, she was smoking cigarettes and watching Scooby Do Where Are You with Tracy.

Or, more likely, she was on the couch, sound asleep.

I felt like having Rose pull over so I could call her and wake her up.

"I have meatloaf sandwiches and some soup on the stove," Rose said. "Bob and Margie are going to be happy to see you, Cal. They talked about you boys all last night, the way they raised you boys there."

I had to eat, I knew that, but I was nervous at the thought of sitting at Rose's dinette over bowls of soup, looking into my parents' haggard faces, and to tell you the truth, I didn't even feel hungry.

"Sounds good," I said.

SMILING, MY PARENTS MET US in the hallway. My father was wearing clothes too big for him: my uncle's golf pants, a fuzzy cardigan, and a shirt with a flying mallard embroidered on the pocket. My mother had a new hairstyle. She was wearing lipstick. She was dressed in a bathrobe. Dad grabbed my hand between his and kissed me.

"God it's good to see you," he said.

I hugged them both at the same time.

"You look fine, Cal," my mother said. "How are the girls?"

"They're fine. They feel bad about all this. Trina couldn't get away. They're sorry they couldn't make it."

"We think the world of those two," my mother said. "You know that." She kissed me and smiled.

"So how's the plant?" asked Dad.

I told him I was a packaging supervisor now. "It was easy," I said. "I just showed them how to stack more hotdog buns in a carton."

My parents laughed.

We went into the kitchen and crowded into the dinette. Rose brought sandwiches on a plate and set cups of soup in front of us. We ate quietly and slowly, some birds flying around the feeder in the falling snow outside the window. My parents were bearing up, though their shoulders slumped.

My father put down his spoon. "Woke up at three thirty," he said, lining the spoon up with the flashing pattern of vinyl gingham covering Rose's dinette. "Air sucking down the hallway, it's a funny sound. Rumbling at the other end of the house." He looked at the spoon. "Makes me sick to think about it."

"We went out the bathroom window," my mother said. "We watched it from the lawn."

"It's a shame," I said.

"It was a good house," my father said, looking at me.

"Great house," I said. "Beautiful house."

"Like a bonfire," said my mother. "All the photographs are gone."

Rose poured coffee. We fixed our cups the way we like them, my father moving his spoon back and forth, stirring.

"We went back for some things," he said. "But there isn't much. It's out in the garage. Make sure you go help yourself."

I shook my head no.

He took me anyway. I looked at what they had salvaged, spread out on a sheet—lumps, cinders, warped and tarnished objects. I picked out two curled-up spoons and the head of a hammer I had used as a kid, but back in the kitchen Rose turned from her sink and informed me that what I had chosen was already spoken for, by her. She seemed kind of excited about it, so I let it pass.

Then she and my mother washed dishes while my father and I went into the living room. He stood by the fireplace, holding on to the mantle with one hand. He looked smaller than he really is, in my uncle's clothes.

"How's your car running?" he asked.

"Jumped time," I said. "Backfires. I drive through town, it sounds like the bank's being robbed."

He smiled.

"The Olds shimmies at fifty-five," he said. "Can't get it out."

"Idler arm," I said.

He nodded, stooping. Then he said "Oh my Lord," something I had never heard him say before, and he looked down, shaking his head, and then up, smiling, and said, "We lost that too. That burned up too."

Then his smile was gone and he told me, "There's just some things you can't control. You can't control them. You just have to accept them."

I nodded.

"The past is past, and you can't fix it. There isn't anything you can do about it," he said. He was staring at me. "Never forget to be happy for what you have," he said. "Me, I have a loving wife and I have two healthy sons, both who turned out good. I'm lucky," he said. "I thank God."

I thought of Wayne, who was probably doing a labirynthectomy or a radical neck dissection as we spoke. Then my father walked up to me and faced me square. He said, "I've been though the war. I saw the floating dead out in the channel. I saw our own bombers breaking up under the flak and going down in flames. Our ships, loaded with men, hitting Jerrie mines and sinking in a few minutes."

He sat on the couch and stared at the carpet. He said, "They just died."

Then my mother and aunt came in and we tried to find something on TV.

But nothing was on and we sat in silence until I began to feel a rolling anxiety.

"Can I borrow the Cutlass?" I asked. "I'll be back for dinner and we can call Wayne."

MY FIRST STOP WAS THE HOUSE, which as you would imagine was just a cement foundation in the snow. Nothing was left but the basement itself, a bowl of cinders with snow over them, yet I had the feeling that underneath, down in there, something had to be left. As I looked down, I thought of throwing darts, and the dartboard we had all played with, and I got to wondering what ever happened to it. It was something I had never thought about before, I realized, and it was creepy, because I kept seeing us throwing darts down there and eating popcorn, my parents all energetic and everybody having fun, and I kept wondering what could have happened to it. I wanted to know. I wanted to account for it. It had to be somewhere.

Twilight came while I stood there, snow blowing around. Then it got dark and grey.

Finally, I left.

I drove to the High-Lo. Nobody was there that I knew, and it gave me an eerie feeling to be a stranger where I once had been such a steady and respected customer. Still, I stayed a couple hours to watch a Piston's game and drink Seven and Sevens. Then it began to seem familiar. It smelled beery, and they still had the shuffleboard game with its long, slippery alley, its clack of game pieces and tinkling bells. They had the same pool tables, even, dirty and worn by now. The bathroom was still cold.

By the time the game was over I had finished drinking and was ready to go home. Outside it was dark and cold, clear, the snowing stopped, a few stars in the sky. I headed to Aunt Rose's, worried it was still too early. On the way I passed the Rollatorium and saw its sign lit up. I wouldn't have thought it would still be in business.

Inside it was the same colored lights and top-forty music and roar of roller skates. I sat on a smooth bench. The kids circled one way, then changed directions, then skated girls only and then boys only, as per the instructions of the disc jockey, just as I had done nearly every weekend when I was growing up in Cadillac. They went by like a herd of gazelles under the colored lights.

I watched for maybe twenty minutes and then I left.

I bought a Snickers on my way out. As I crossed the parking lot I saw something I hadn't seen in a long time but which didn't surprise me at all, a fight. They were squaring off with the crowd around them. They were just kids. One of them was still wearing his skates. They were fools. I wanted them to stop. I stepped between them to break it up. I told them to knock it off.

"Get lost," said the skater.

"Go fuck yourself," said the other. They went into it like hockey players, the crowd watching.

I watched, too, for a moment, then I walked to the Cutlass and started it and sat there in the lot with the motor running, trying to understand what I was doing there. I sat there until the heat was blasting and the inside of the car was so hot I couldn't breathe.

On the way back to Rose's I thought about calling Wayne. Instead I stopped for a pint of Seagram's. Outside the store, I called Trina.

"They're okay," I said.

"That's good," Trina said. "How are you?"

"I'm okay too."

"Honey," she said. "C'mon home. We'll be waiting at the station at four."

"Is Tracy okay?" I asked.

"She's fine. She's going to a birthday party tomorrow."

"Okay," I said. "I'll see you tomorrow."

I imagined them waiting for me.

While my brother was in med school, I was driving a bread truck around Cadillac, and I was none too sure of myself, to say the least. Then, about the time the frustration started turning to fear, I got transferred to Evansville, which I learned is a good city, a city of equals. It's where I met Trina. She was a nurse's aide then, and she still is. We don't have much money, but we have good lives.

IT WAS LATE WHEN I GOT IN, and everyone was in bed. I tried to watch an Abbot and Costello movie but I had seen it a number of times and wasn't entertained. I went to my room, which had been my cousin Doug's. The bed and bureau had wagon wheels on them, the walls done up with wallpaper cowboys riding and branding and shooting.

Dougie had messed around when he was a kid, breaking into the IGA for beer, skipping school, so Rose sent him to the Howe School for Boys, a military academy in Kansas. He ran away once or twice at first, sent me letters saying they beat him with paddles, but eventually he got straightened around, learned to get along and studied hard, and started coming home for vacations in a snappy dress uniform that I envied. When he graduated he became a lieutenant in the Army right away and went to Vietnam, which was the end of him.

I drank the whiskey. I lay there, listening to my mother cry in the next room until the other noises in the house and out on the street had long since ceased.

In the morning we had eggs and bacon and we talked about what kind of house they would like to get and where, and I said I would visit.

"I want to buy some clothes," Dad said, and they took me to the station.

RIDING BACK TO EVANSVILLE, I remembered the times I had been in trains:

When I was ten, a friend and I took a train to Chicago and back again, just for the ride.

During my high school senior trip, in Mexico, some friends and I were riding somewhere on a train when a woman in our car died. That train stopped, right in the middle of nowhere.

Now I was on a train going back home to Evansville. I was going back to the Bunny Bread factory and I was going home to Trina and Tracy. In South Bend we took on passengers. A young woman sat facing me the rest of the trip.

She was going home after a two-week rendezvous with her lover.

She cried all the way to Evansville.

"Stop this train," she kept saying.

GRIP

SNOW WAS STILL FALLING—it had fallen all night—though by now the drifting had stopped. It was me, Hastings, Kleinbrook, and John West—wading through the drifts, sinking steel poles around a field so we could string a wire on them and hook the ends to an electric fence generator in the horse barn. Some guy that Hastings knew was supposed to give us each a case of Budweiser when we finished. You could see the horses, watching us from the barn.

One guy holds the fence pole. It's straight as a rail, with a bracket riveted to it about half way down, a steel plate that crosses at right angles and sticks out a couple inches either side. Two guys lift a cast-iron pipe over the end of the pole, and they slide that heavy pipe up and down, driving it against the bracket, nailing the pole into the ground. And that's what we were doing—thump, thump, thumping it down—when John West caught his hand between the bracket and the pipe. It made a clean sound.

"Oh jeez" John West whipped his hand off the pole. He clamped his glove under his left armpit and yanked out his hand, throwing a loop of blood onto the fresh snow around us and sending his ring finger flying. It landed silent, sunk in a snowdrift.

John West grabbed his wrist with his left hand and squeezed.

"Let's get to the hospital," Hastings said.

"Take his finger," Kleinbrook said, but we couldn't find it. It was lost in all that fluffy snow.

"Fuck it," said John West. Blood was shooting like a hose from his knuckle. We got in the car.

It had been our misfortune for this to take place out in the sticks. It made for a long ride to the hospital, snow blowing across the roads, the car creeping along with John West holding his hand bleeding in his lap. I was worried. I was afraid the life would drain out of him right there in the front seat.

"You're going to be fine, Johnny-boy," Hastings said, which made me feel better, though John West didn't say anything to it.

Kleinbrook said, "Ever been to the hospital, John?"

John West didn't say anything.

"Well I have," he said, "and you know what? They don't have the slightest idea what they're doing. I fell out of an apple tree when I was twelve, you know? And broke my arm? So my old man drives me down there, and the bone's poking my skin up, and we sit in the waiting room for two hours because he doesn't have insurance."

Hastings leaned forward, driving.

"I mean, come on," Kleinbrook said. "My arm's hanging off, and I can't feel it anymore, and they're walking around, drinking coffee behind the counter and telling jokes. Christ. So finally they sit me in this little wheelchair and they roll me into a room, and then they leave me there."

I tapped his knee. I shook my head "No" when he looked at me.

But he went on.

"I'm holding my arm, you know, and this guy comes in, and he pushes my hand away and he grabs my wrist and starts pulling! Just pulls my arm straight out, and keeps pulling! Oh man, that hurt. I said, 'Hey, motherfucker, stop, goddamn it,' and this guy goes, 'That didn't hurt.' The hell it didn't."

"Shut up, Terry," I said. "I mean it."

It was like driving at night then, a feeling of darkness in the car, heater fan blowing and snow everywhere. I sat behind John West. He had long blond hair like a girl's and it hung down snarled and wet and never moved. He was wearing a Levi's jacket. I was good and scared.

WHILE THEY LOOKED AT JOHN WEST in the emergency room, I sat in a dark blue chair in the waiting room thinking about the time he mowed lawns with us in Ann Arbor. He'd kept his face down the whole time, his long hair hanging around it, blond, so you could never see him in there. And he was quiet. He kept saying "Thank you." Hand him a gas can, he'd say, "Thank you." Help him unload a mower, "Thank you."

Then a doctor came into the waiting room and said they were closing the wound and giving John West a blood transfusion. They were going to keep him overnight to monitor his electrolyte levels and do some EEG's, the doctor said. John West was unconscious and needed rest, the doctor said. We went home.

They released John West two days later. I hadn't gone to visit him while he was in the hospital, because I wanted to forget it. I figured he would go his own way and I would probably never see him again. That was how I wanted it to be. Then one Saturday afternoon, after the snow had melted, before the buds had broken and everything was wet with runoff, I came on him stalled on the river road, down on a bend where the road touches the water.

He was holding the hood up with his left hand, his damaged right lying with its missing finger across the top of the air cleaner, strange and mysterious, like a magical sign, as if he were putting a hex on the motor, or trying to, with that hand. Then I saw he was only thinking, as if by pressing his hand on the air cleaner, he could read the motor's mind.

"Started missing, then just quit," he said through all his hair.

I nosed the trucks together and we hooked up booster cables, but it was useless. John West cranked and cranked the ignition, but the motor wouldn't start. I kept trying, though. I tried everything. I pulled the air cleaner and the plugs, checked to see he was getting fuel and spark, I made sure he wasn't flooded, I had him crank and crank the starter until, finally, the engine backfired though the carb, shooting fire. I balled up my jacket and smothered the flames.

"Maybe you jumped time," I told him and backed my truck up to his. I tied the booster cables between our bumpers so I could tow him to Tiny's.

The cables stretched as I pulled him there, John West drifting farther and farther away, his head in the rearview mirror getting smaller and smaller as I towed him. By the time we got to Tiny's he was way back, twenty feet behind me, the cables sagging, thin as an extension cord.

I walked to his truck with a hacksaw to cut the cables free, but before I could get there, he was kneeling at his bumper, trying to untie the knot. It was hard and tight, but he kept clawing at it.

I turned around and went to my truck, where I was sawing through the cables tight around my bumper, when he came up behind me and handed them to me, all coiled up, even though they were shot.

"Thank you," he said.

Tiny's brother watched us from inside the glass front of the station. When we went in he told us nobody was there to look at John West's truck, so we left it, and I drove John West home. He directed me through parts of town I'd never been before, down back streets, through little neighborhoods, saying "You want to go left here" or "Keep going straight," to a house on a cul-de-sac in a subdivision of split-levels. I pulled into the driveway expecting him to roll out and say "Thank you," but to my surprise, he offered me a beer.

It was a big, family house, but it was empty. I mean, there was nothing there at all—no furniture, no pictures on the walls, no rugs, no lamps, no curtains. Nothing. Just floors, walls, electrical outlets, and ceilings, all the same pale yellow, a misty light coming in the windows. I followed him into the kitchen. He opened the refrigerator and brought out two cans of Stroh's and an open canned ham. He slid one of the beers toward me then cut blocks of ham, pointing at mine with the knife. We leaned on the counter eating the chunks and drinking beer.

"So where is everybody?" I asked.

"Gone," he said. "Some guys from the pallet factory rented with me here, but the owner wanted us out. They left."

I nodded.

He took me upstairs to a bedroom. There was his stuff—a bed, a Voice of Music stereo, an acoustic guitar with two strings on it, his clothes in a pile, a jar full of pennies. He had a sleeping bag, tangled on the mattress of his bed. He showed me a baby cactus in a potpie tin on the windowsill, then a goldfish in a yellow plastic dishpan. I was watching the fish hover in the middle of thetub, its tiny fins fanning, when the door opened downstairs.

"That's Hugh," John West said. "The owner." We listened as Hugh walked across the living room floor to the bottom of the stairs. The boards creaked. "John?" he yelled up.

We went down and I met the guy. He looked like he had some money, but he was nice enough.

"I'm going to be painting the upstairs, John," he said, "and you got to go now."

So I told John West he could stay with me if he wanted.

To tell you the truth, I was happy he moved in. I was living in a little house out in the country, a place on the road to Saline I had shared for three years with Rod Bell. But Bell was gone, married, and I couldn't afford it alone. It certainly was worth trying to afford. There were birches on the front lawn you could watch from a glassed-in porch, and out back, a cement slab patio overlooked a marsh and some low hills that went off into the farthest distance under the big Michigan sky. You could see deer out there in the mornings, and from time to time a fox, or great blue heron, and when the sun set, the whole place lit up in curtains of purple and red and lemon yellows, the fields warm and glowing, until there was nothing you could do but sit there and watch it all fade as the emptiness of night came down. I was afraid I would have to move into a trailer. But John West and I kept it. Together we covered the bills.

He was as quiet as a mouse, but we got along, and between the two of us, we had a good spring. We started some marijuana seedlings in egg cartons under the sunlight on the glassed-in porch, and when the weather warmed up, we changed the windows to screens, and hid the plants out in the hills. We went on long walks through the fields, bringing milk jugs to water the marijuana, or sometimes just to roam. We followed the stream through the woods. We found an old, lopsided barn out in the green grass of an overgrown field, inside of which was a rotting, sway-backed travel trailer, inside of which, in a kitchen drawer, we found a flat mahogany case filled with hundreds of little magnifying glasses with tiny handles on them all stacked in slots—"tester-lenses for an eye doctor," John West said. We kept a few to fool with; the rest we scattered around.

That spring, John West helped me convert my GMC to dual exhausts. We worked together on lots of things. We took turns cooking supper—John West specializing in pre-packaged spaghetti dinner kits; me, burritos—with whoever wasn't cooking that night doing the dishes. We went in on a cable hook-up and watched old reruns—Rawhide, Car 54 Where Are You? Dirty Harry. He brought home strips of wood from the pallet factory and we made a box kite, six feet tall, covered with shopping bag paper, which we flew on nylon binding twine 600 yards into the April winds. We made beer.

We threw parties for ourselves, inviting guys from the pallet factory and the aluminum plant, parties that lasted all night. There would be people in our living room in the morning, sleeping, guys neither John West nor I knew, but nice guys, and we'd feed them corn flakes and drive them downtown.

One night we fixed ourselves up, combed our hair, shined our boots, and went to Big Daddy's. That was the night we met the girls.

They came home with us after last rounds and stayed three days. Janice worked data processing at Detroit Ball Bearing. She was five feet tall and good looking, full of energy all the time. She told me she once owned a Harley Davidson that she drove to the laundromat. She said that when she was five years old, she had been the star of the Niles, Michigan, Veteran's Day Parade. Dressed up in a cowgirl uniform, she went riding down the street on a black horse, leading all the bands. Her parents died in a car crash when she was three and she had grown up with her grandfather, who told her she was "the best girl in the world."

She was separated from her husband, who was in Florida, and who, I believe, she wanted to go back to, though she knew she never would. I never found out how old she was, but it didn't matter. Her smile was a beautiful thing to see, and she had a swagger in her small voice that meant she was looking out for number one. I liked her a lot.

John West, though, fell in love those first three days. Mona, her name was—short for Ramona. She was dark-eyed and tall and had a way of sitting across the room with her legs crossed, her eyes half-lidded and sliding while she jerked and moved and waved that leg, saying something by it. She liked to drink and dance. She was good at poker and she beat us every time. She had John West in a state.

It got so they were coming over Fridays after work, staying the weekend, and sometimes into the week. We did everything together, like a family. We'd all go to Pizza Hut, where it was easy to see how much John West was in love by the way he did all the talking. He was going to trade his truck in on a Camaro, or he was going to get his own place, or Ramona, do you want some mints, do you want another beer? I can't say there was anything bad about it. It was good to see him having a good time, and they were happy. We were all happy.

THEN THE BREEZY, SPRINGTIME trees all went bitter green and dusty and still with summer, and it was hot out, hot the night that me and Janice came home from bowling and heard John West and Ramona yelling up in his room. We could hear them as we walked across the yard. When the screen door slapped behind us, they shut up, and we didn't hear any more from them that night, but the next morning, on the kitchen counter, the sugar bowl was upside-down, and under the pile of sugar was a note, "Goodbye."

John West started moping around the house after that. It made the place feel like an attic.

"Oh, man. This is worse than having your dog get hit by a car," he said one afternoon, finally, trying to shake the blues.

But he couldn't shake them. They wouldn't let go. He started heating TV dinners when it was his turn to cook, and I lost my appetite, but I ate them anyway. Then he stopped watching cable with me. After a while, he didn't eat with me at all. He just went silent again. He accepted voluntary overtime at the pallet factory and went into his room when he got home. He sat on the cement stoop all through the weekends, drinking and chainsmoking marijuana.

"Get your shit together, bub," I finally told him one night as he brooded out on the cement stoop. "Stop taking it so hard."

He got up and went to his bedroom.

I sat out there with the stars filling the sky over my head for I don't know how long, until I realized he had come back and was standing in the doorway without saying anything.

It scared me.

"Let's go get ice cream sandwiches," he said, silhouetted by the light from the kitchen.

"Okay," I said, "that'd be a good idea," and we drove toward town, past the viaduct, heading to the Dairy Queen. But he veered off, out onto FH Avenue, which cuts through the farmlands around Niles and eventually turns to dirt. We rode without talking, our windows down, moths zinging white lines in the empty road in front of us. Then he shut off the headlights and coasted the truck to a stop across the street from a ranch house, and we sat there. John West looked into the windows. He leaned forward on the steering wheel and stared into the house.

"I wonder what she's doing in there," he said.

"Oh," I said. We sat in the truck looking at the orange light coming from the house. "Well," I said after a while, "I think we better get out of here."

On the way home, I told John West he should go easy on himself. Just let it go. Move on.

He didn't answer. In the glow of the dashboard lights, he just looked sore.

The next day he came home from the factory with the biggest bottle of Chivas Regal they make. He was in a grand mood. He said, "Let's grill chicken, man! Let's get loaded!" He was tipping the bottle back, taking big slugs. "C'mon," he said, "let's have a good time. Fuck it!"

We'd started the charcoal and were throwing the frisbee out on the front lawn when he stepped down onto the road, where the cars slingshot around the curve for the trip to Saline. I remember him reaching for the disc, his body all stretched out. I remember his leg spinning around and the way the sound flopped off the front of the house when the car hit him. It knocked him onto the grass. The bastard didn't stop. I called the ambulance.

John West spent nine days in the hospital was all, even though he had a broken pelvis, a fractured jaw, a dislocated shoulder, and a ruptured diaphram. His insurance company paid for the surgery and arranged for a visiting nurse to take care of him after that.

They sent him home. They gave him a subsidy to recuperate there. I set him up on the screened-in porch at the front of the little house. If you've never taken care of somebody who is really sick, then you probably don't know how lucky you are just to walk down the street. It was hot out on the porch, but John West would lie there shuddering, shivering in his sleep, a voice in every breath. I parked a chair beside him and I'd sit there, listening to him wake just long enough to roll his eyes and say, "I'm sick," or "Help," or "Oh." His nurse's name was Vi. She came every morning. A metal bracket went through the skin of John West's hips and held his pelvis clamped together with screws. His cast went around his stomach and down to his knees.

I KNEW JANICE DIDN'T LIKE coming around so much, John West lying there like that. I wasn't fun when we went out, and wouldn't dance. She called me one night and told me how much she liked me, said we were friends and always would be, but after that I didn't hear from her anymore, though at times, when the phone rang, I would hope.

I did the best I could. I came home from work at lunchtime and fixed him oatmeal and grape juice. I sat on the porch, and we ate, then I made sure he could reach the phone, and I left him water and drove back to the plant. In the afternoons he sat idle, looking out the porch screens at the clouds going by or at cars at the end of the drive. You could hear them punch the accelerator as they took the curve, heading for Saline. I'd come home from work and we'd have dinner. I fixed his favorite, mashed fish sticks and creamed corn, banana pudding and ice cream. I moved the TV out there and we watched it. I'd sit out there with him until he fell asleep again.

His payments came in and we covered the expenses. I worked, and when I got home I took care of him. I washed the sweat from his face and his arms and his chest. I changed his bed pan. I clipped the fingernails from his damaged hand and from his good one. I shaved him and brushed his teeth, I clipped his toenails and gave him a haircut. I cut the stringy hair out of his eyes.

John West lay in the bed on the screened-in porch, day and night, the rest of the summer. We watched the sky over Saline light up in streaks of pastel color on the Fourth of July. We watched thunderstorms from the porch, or some nights just fireflies. The nights went cool and I put the windows back, and then we watched through the glass as the trees turned rusty, red, then tinged gold and purple with fall.

He was healing fast, and he could play cards and chew, and he was talking, talking about walking again and going to the bathroom by himself, talking about getting his cast off. Vi'd come and do his tests—blood tests, urine tests which showed he was stable—she'd give him his meds and help me change his bed. She and I were having coffee in the kitchen one morning when she said John West was lucky to have somebody like me to take care of him.

She said John West was lucky considering how bad he had been hurt. She said he was lucky just to be alive.

"One thing's for sure," she said. "He won't ever run again."

She couldn't have been more right about that. When John West got his cast off, he could barely walk.

He hobbled like a chicken.

He went back to work at the pallet factory, like before, but of course, it was nothing like it had been between us. We didn't drink or smoke so much anymore. We had no desire to throw down like before. We only took it easy. Something had been scraped out of him by it all.

Instead, we took long walks in the hills. We just took walks, farther and farther away from the house and into the fall countryside. Somebody had found most of the pot; it didn't matter. John West liked to wander through the woods beyond the hills, roaming, getting lost. I had my father's .22 and a Savage 20-gauge shotgun, and we took them with us. John West had never hunted before, but it got to where we were taking the guns out every night, walking out back, over the hills and through the wavy oaks and disjointed birch trees to the hardwoods to scare up rabbit for the 20-gauge, or sometimes just to sit on different sides of a hollow, where John West could shoot squirrel down the sights of the .22.

It was times like these, when we sat out in the woods, little places where the wind blew through the trees and John West disappeared into the bushes, that I would look up into the leaves, shotgun across my lap, thinking about how Michigan is a beautiful, strange place, how if you grow up here, like I did, you can never leave. I had known people who tried—Tom King went to California, stopped in Las Vegas, sent post cards saying he won two hundred bucks, sent cards from California, too, about the sun and mountains, but he came back in a year and a half, saying, "I just like Michigan."

But if you haven't grown up in Michigan, then you can't take it, and eventually, you will have to go. This is why my mother and father and brother went back to Arkansas when I was sixteen. I grew up in Michigan, they didn't. That's why they left, and I can't go.

And I suppose that's why John West had to go, too, why he told me one Saturday afternoon that he was leaving.

WE WERE WATCHING a curling championship on TV. Guys were sliding rocks down long alleys of ice.

"What do you mean, you're leaving?"

"I want to get out of here," he said.

"Oh," I said. "Where you going?"

"North Carolina."

"North Carolina?" It was ridiculous. "What's in North Carolina?"

He hung his head. "I don't know. I just like it there."

"You like it there? You ever even been there?"

"No . . . I don't know."

"Well, hell. What, you just saw it on the Andy Griffith show?"

"Listen, I don't have to explain myself," he said.

"Neither do I," I told him. "You aren't going."

He laughed. "Who says?"

"I do. God damn it, I'm telling you not to go."

"Yeah well," he said, "I'm sorry, man, but I'm gonna."

"Well," I told him, "you think about it a while."

"Nope."

"God damn it," I said, "you can't just leave like this."

"Why can't I?"

"Because, I'm telling you. I don't want you to."

We sat there silent, the TV flashing patterns.

"That's crazy," I said.

"What do you mean, crazy? Hey, man, I came here from Vancouver. That was no crazier than going down there's gonna be. It'll be a lot less."

We didn't discuss it after that, and then, on a Saturday morning one week later, he walked into the kitchen and said, "Well, this is it."

I didn't say anything. What could I say? I watched him carry his guitar and some boxes of clothes to his truck and put them in the bed. He was wearing a pair of bluejeans that used to be mine.

I went out to the driveway. I said, "Man, just don't leave, for Christsakes. Why don't you just stick it out? What the hell am I supposed to do now?"

He said, "That, I don't know, man. I'm just not hanging around here, anymore, and that's all."

"Listen," I said. "C'mon. Don't."

"Don't what?"

"Don't go."

He shook his head.

I said, "Okay. Then have a cup of coffee with me before you leave." I felt like I was begging. I followed him back to the kitchen. I poured us coffee. He tipped his cup back and drained it, and put it on the table. He smiled at me.

"Well, man," he said. "Thank you."

He stuck his hand out, across the table, and my heart jumped, and my hand lifted and grabbed his, my fingers wrapping around the edge of his palm into the cavity where his finger should have been, and I mean to tell you, it was a bad feeling.

I'D COME HOME from the aluminum plant, and the sun would be going down, the days turning shorter and shorter for winter coming on, and I could see the sun set through the windows in the glassed-in porch, through the rooms inside the house, through the picture window in the back—all lined up together—I could see the sun through the empty house. It got colder. The winds came, stripping the trees, and they blew right through me, then left, the trees flat like shattered glass against the hard Michigan sky.

THREE WEEKS LATER it was snowing like mad. The power had gone out and I was sitting in the kitchen with a blanket hanging over the door, all four burners going on the stove. I had dragged an armchair in there. I wasn't doing anything, just sitting in the blue light listening to the fluttering of the gas flames, when the phone rang.

It was John West. He was in North Carolina. It was okay, there were magnolia trees, and he had a job already in a little firm that manufactured staple guns for surgeons. He was staying in his truck until he found a place. I told him about the snow and the power being out. He said he'd write once he got settled in.

SUSPECTS WANTED

TEN MINUTES INTO HIS SHIFT, Officer Cody is running to his car, his keys and cases, cuffs, nightstick, and walkie-talkie slapping. It's lost, blended in with the rest of the swarm of shiny blue and white Plymouth Fury Salons in the station lot, until he spots the little red digits painted over a rear quarterpanel, 633. He flings his clipboard inside and sits down with a grunt, reels the seatbelt across his belly, and turns wide out of the lot onto Howard, flooring it. The exhausts hammer. The car goes whipping through traffic, sixty, seventy miles per hour, rear wheels spinning free over every icy patch on the road, yelping as they snap back into traction. Cody's got his lights going.

The radio rasps an ongoing dispatch. It's Domestic Violence again—some woman with a baseball bat busting out the windows of her husband's car at their residence on the far edge of Cody's patrol. Two other cars are already en route. Car 633 drives like a fighter jet honing in on its target. Its motor is tuned as tight as a banjo string. Cody's on his way.

It's a trip into the boonies. Cody's riding through the passage between daytime and night and his whirling lights color the trunks of trees alongside the road, their branches going up inky into the sky. A snowflake pierces the light surrounding the speeding car, then veers up, gone. Beside him in the dimness, Cody's clipboard has skidded its tickets, sheets, and forms all across the seat. He'll straighten them later. He could turn on the siren, but that would make a light flash on the dashboard, telling him it's on, which would be absurd. The fan blows heated air.

Cody's wearing a bullet-stopping vest under his shirt, and it feels tight. He's thinking how, sooner or later, he's gonna have to lose some weight.

The other cars are in the driveway when Cody arrives, their beacons sparkling the neighborhood like confetti. Cody shuts his rack off and coasts up slowly beside a bank of trees at the edge of the yard.

He reports his arrival. Monitor outside, dispatch says, and the radio goes silent.

Cody watches the other two officers and the couple in the living room through the house's picture window from the darkness of the car. He gathers his papers with his arm. He sees the man and woman, standing, yelling at the officer at the same time. They are waving their arms.

The officer standing, Cody knows him from weapons training class. The other, sitting on the couch taking notes, Cody can only see the back of his head. A boy wearing pajamas enters the room. He starts talking, awed by the police, and everyone listens. His hair's all messed. He stretches his arms out too.

A blast of static blows the silence away. Dispatch wants Cody back at the fire station. He's left for patrol without the official go-ahead from Scheduling. The Chief's upset. "10-4," Cody returns the call, but instead of leaving, he gets out of the car. He can tell the situation's under control inside the house, but he goes in to clear with the other officers first, anyway.

The house is warm inside. The man and the woman look tired, sitting on the couch hunched over, panting. Somebody's been baking cinnamon rolls. The kid looks up at Cody like he's going to get some answer. Cody sits on the ottoman next to him and sticks out his red-haired hand. "Howdy partner," he says. The kid looks at Cody's hand, grabs it, and they shake. Nobody here wants to press charges.

Cody heads back to the station through the darkness of the winter night. No moon out: the car cuts through the black of the back roads. The fan blows heat, the radio whispers its litany.

A sensation like too much horseradish hits Cody in the face. He hits the steering wheel with the heel of his hand. This job was a gift from God. Cops do things other people would pay money to be able to do. Whether you're an accountant or a factory worker, you don't have anything to look forward to or worry about when you go to work. Cops have both. It's like doing drugs.

He thrives on it, on the intensity of it, on the intensity of every moment. He gets to be there when the house burns down. He gets to see people hurting. He wants to stand over the heaving chest of a burglar, still feeling the hot air rushing out the broken window. He enjoys going into a riot on the street where people are walking around with ballbats and crowbars, arresting them, bringing peace to the whole neighborhood.

Cody enjoys beating them at their own game!

"All right!" he says out loud. "What a night this is!"

The town spreads out. Cody passes the water tower and golf course and the strip malls surrounding Three Ponds, where Sears used to be.

Yesterday Jan pointed a spatula at him and accused him of living three lives at once. That's how she put it.

She meant Cody lives three times faster than regular people. Cody's a veteran of the force, eleven years. Rookies burn out in four. Eighty percent of them get divorces in their first three. All the women are divorced. He used to like to hunt, but being a cop, you get the same enjoyment. He's got other hobbies now. He likes photography and attending Marriage Encounter sessions. But Fridays aren't date nights anymore.

The streets are dark and it's cold out. He's getting a little hungry. Cody has low blood sugar. His doctor wants him to have something light to eat from time to time.

Cody extends his fingers around the steering wheel and grips.

The trouble with this job, it's like a mistress.

You pay a price for it.

A FINE DRY SNOW IS FALLING. Cody sits in the fire station parking lot while dispatch juggles calls from two other stations who think he's supposed to be with them tonight. It's lonely, sitting in car 633 with its overinflated radials, 318 cubic inch V-8, and 12 gauge Winchester clamped to the dash on the rider's side all by yourself without going anywhere. It's ridiculous.

Snow melted from engine heat leaves a pattern on the hood.

He never used to just sit there. This Merger is two years old. They still don't have it figured out. The police used to meet at the Cop Shop downtown; they'd share stories and kid each other in the locker room before briefing; they had a ritual. Everybody'd leave at the same time, heading out on the different patrols, and it was a smooth operation, no snags—but now everybody meets in tiny groups at the fire stations around town, and nobody ever knows what's going on. Ever since the City Manager dreamed up the Merger, with cops and firefighters alternating responsibilities under the shared designation "Public Safety Officer," nobody knows what they're supposed to do anymore.

Snow crystals clot around the windshield edges, pile on the wipers.

He pops a bread stick from the bulk foods section at Jewel into his mouth and dates and signs the forms on his seat. He'll fill out the rest of them later. If they ever stop making paper, the police will go out of business. He clips the papers in his clipboard, sets it next to him on the seat, where the forms will eventually slip free and skid around all night.

If he ever gets out of here.

He sits waiting for the decision. He waits for half an hour.

Sometimes it gets lonely, but he's used to being alone. He's patrolled the seven PM to seven AM shift by himself for the past six years. Sometimes he takes Jan along, or the department chaplain. Usually it's a firefighter he has to train in police work. Cody's stomach hurts a little. In the trunk of 633, he realizes, are his rubber boots and fire hat and slicker and mask that stink like a little kid's raincoat.

He drops his officer's cap behind the seatback. He may look a tad heavy, but anybody would with a protective vest under their uniform.

There's nothing to do. He unbuttons his pocket flap and takes out his memo pad. It's leafy, worn, he flips the pages—secret, magic, profuse with symbols and dates and stars. He's not supposed to keep personal records, but on the blank page, he writes "Friday, Feb 16," and below that, inks a circle with an "X" through it: One Domestic Assault. He usually tallies the night's events at the end of the shift, remembering each incident in order. The memo pad feels almost sacred in his hands.

He buttons it away. He could go for a hamburger and a cup of coffee right about now, if they didn't cause so much heart disease.

Dispatch clears him then cancels the call before he can drop the car into drive. Then they tell him to report to the Oakland station, but cancel that call right away, too. Then they tell him to go to Oakland and cancel again. Finally they say someone has decided Cody was at the right place all along, so Cody waits, then acknowledges, logs in "8:11" on his clipboard, and pulls slowly across the lot.

Out of the glare of the mercury vapor lights, in a dark, snowy corner, Cody stops the car. He presses his back into the seat and lowers his head. His eyes shut. They roll into the back of his head. "Father, keep me from pride tonight, that I may do right. I ask that you watch me and protect me. Father, thank you for this day which you have created for us. Be with my family while I am away. In Jesus' name, Amen."

Then he pulls out of the lot, heading for patrol.

AH, WHAT'S BECOME OF THIS TOWN? Cody used to fish for carp in the Three Ponds with sugar-and-dough balls. Now there's probably no fish there at all. There probably aren't even weeds left.

He sweeps Area Six from one end to the other, 633 cruising briskly.

The city's like a landing strip. Empty.

He watches for traffic violators and listens to the radio. Nothing.

Well, the weirdos aren't out yet. Give 'em time.

He drives around the neighborhoods writing parking tickets for a while. He finds a whole row of illegally parked cars. A few streets over, a pick-up parked at a diagonal in a no parking zone, three feet from the curb, facing traffic. Ticket. Old snow crunches under Cody's feet. He turns the collar of his jacket up. This cold is solid. He holds his hands over his ears.

It's as good a time as any to run up to Greenbriar Estates, the apartment complex, and serve a subpoena. A twenty minute drive. 633 is nice and warm inside.

Cody hopes the kid's in. The guy who owns the place has a big pile of garbage in the back yard, garbage he won't take to the dump, and the kid, a renter, doesn't want to testify against his landlord. Cody knocks on the door and waits.

The kid answers, awfully surprised. He looks guilty, blinking.

"Relax," says Cody. "That you?" Pointing to the name.

"Yeah . . . "

"Here."

The subpoena lays in the kid's hand like a fish. "What's this?"

Cody smiles. "You have to go to court," he says. The words are satisfying to say. "Don't worry about it."

Cody heads down the warm hallway. The way he looks at it, God put us here to prove that we can do right. Sometimes Cody looks at some of these people and he just wants to ask them, "Why are you breathing and taking up space?" But Cody's a born-again Christian. He has to stop and remind himself that the Lord looked into their futures and was willing to die for them. He put them here for a reason! Cody loves people, and he wants to give as much comfort and peace and justice and order as he can, but he wants to see them live up to their potential, even if it means locking them up. It's his calling.

He passes a junker under a mound of snow as big as itself. He stops, digs down to the windshield, puts an abandoned vehicle sticker on it. Getting this job was a miracle, for Cody. He's the only professional in his family! He's the only Cody with a college degree!

633's almost cozy. After stopping at the home of a student who reported her dog stolen only to find she discovered it under the couch just before he arrived, Cody gets a radio call, another car asking him to rendezvous in the employee lot of the WKZO broadcast station.

A SIGN OF NEON LETTERS three feet high flashes "WKZO TV" in green, then "WKZO RA " in red above 633 as Cody works the beam of his spotlight. It hits the other cruiser, down in the shadows with some cars parked off the edge of the lot. Cody drives down and parks farther back, away from the cars of the night employees at the studios, and waits.

Snow is falling, tiny ice crystals. Cody rolls his window down. Cops miss the camaraderie since the merger . . . who can blame them? Cops who don't have to spend their shifts as firefighters wait until they get out on patrol to meet each other for an opportunity to talk. There is something almost clandestine about it. The other patrol car pulls up carefully, coming from the opposite direction: side by side, driver to driver, and slowly, face to face. The officer in the other car is barely visible in the shadows under his roof.

"I haven't seen you for a long time, Dale," Cody says.

"Been working narc for the past three years," Dale says. He stays in the darkness.

"First you've been back?"

"I've been back for about a month, Cam. I even had a briefing with you a couple weeks ago."

"I'm sorry, Dale. I didn't remember."

"They've had me working days," Dale complains.

Dale's face, what Cody can see of it, hovers in the darkness, wan and white.

"Yeah. What area do you have tonight?"

"Seven. I don't like it. I wish I had my old area back. I liked when the old area seven took in Oakwood."

"I know what you mean. I don't even like the architecture out there."

Cody turns the radio down to a whisper. He tips his clipboard into the pale light and starts filling out an abandoned vehicle form.

"Until the 'All-District County-Wide Police/Fire Merger,' I never worked days," Dale says. "I could kill, Cam. This shit I'm seeing is unreal."

"I know. I'm sorry, Dale."

"It reminds me of that training film where the guy rushes into the scene and gets killed because he didn't wait for help," Dale says. "I don't like going out with those guys, Cam. They don't know what they're doing. They're firefighters."

"It's depressing," Cody says.

"You remember this summer, where they surrounded those cops? I was one of them, Cam. I was out in that parking lot, and where were those guys? They didn't show up for twenty minutes, Cam! They even found one of them sleeping in his car!"

"I've been to places where they are, and I tell you, I can feel the fear," Cody says. "I want to stop a block away and call a 10-26 and let 'em know I'm there."

"They slaughtered this job."

"It's an embarrassment."

"They tarnished the badge, Cam."

"I applied to Portage," Cody says in a soft voice.

He looks past the parking lot into the dark, snowy field. Lights twinkle through sticks far away on the other side. He wonders if anybody could possibly be out there tonight.

"We're just out here fighting crime and facing death," Dale says, like a weird joke.

"Yeah," says Cody. They sit in the quiet. Cody could just about cry. Police are some of the best people in the world. You go to any city, you've got a hundred friends.

ONE THING CODY HASN'T HAD in quite a while is a turkey and dressing dinner. He can almost taste it, thick brown gravy running off the whipped potatoes, the pepper, sopping up his plate with Wonderbread.

But then, there'd be all those cholesterols in his blood, jamming up his arteries like calcium in a pipe. Thanks but no thanks!

Hey, the basketball game's letting out at Saint Monica's. Cody imagines all the people happy from having sat together in the big gymnasium watching sports. He passes 633 back and forth in front of the school like a shark, just to make himself visible to any drivers trying to be the first ones out on the street.

Directly under a sign which prohibits it, a Celica makes a left turn. Unbelievable. Cody flips on the rack of lights on the roof and stamps the accelerator flat, careening around the corner. All the cars in the intersection pull to the curbs.

The Celica halts with Cody behind it pointing the spotlight into the rear window. He leaves it there and gets out, thin-lipped.

"I'm a student," the driver says, looking up with big eyes through a face of curly hair. "I just got back from break. I don't know town very well." Cody takes her driver's license and calls it in, filling out her ticket while he waits.

As he is giving her her ticket a car passes with a headlight out. Cody drops the ticket in her hand and runs to his car. Lights on; he leans forward in his seat catching up. The car won't pull over. It's a jacked-up fool-mobile with a sticker that says, "BABY!" across the trunk. Cody crunches a bread stick straight down, riding the car's rear bumper. He floods the passenger compartment with spotlight. The cars almost touch. It pulls over.

The driver tells Cody that 633 has a light out, too—one of the rotating lights on the roof. He's cocky, a little runt with stray black hairs coming from his chin. Cody takes his license and calls dispatch.

Alfonso Real. Military age, minority, or they live at a rented address: Cody calls them in. This guy's name doesn't look right. Dispatch shows no warrants outstanding, so Cody returns Mr. Real's license along with a ticket just in case and thanks him for the information.

Cody's thankful he's got a calling. Just, he doesn't see why cops stay so honest, sometimes. There's no motivation for it. There's no money in it, no promotion. There's no acknowledgement, except maybe from your peers. And the more involved you are, the more you stand to lose! So why do cops keep doing it? They're still honest! They're still motivated! Cody doesn't get it!

Snow's falling in clumpy flakes. He chomps a breadstick. Cops are regular people. They hurt too. It's very ugly sometimes. Cody's seen a family fighting in front of their Christmas tree, hitting each other with the presents. He's seen a child spanked for smiling at him.

A slug of bile backs up in Cody's throat. He is not racially prejudiced. Some of his very best friends are black. But he is culturally prejudiced, he knows that, and why shouldn't he be? He doesn't want his kids hanging around with somebody who walks like a broken chicken. He doesn't want them hanging around with somebody who turns his radio up seven times louder than it needs to be. He doesn't want them hanging around with somebody who drives a car like a moving hotel room!

Cody's living in an abyss he can't get out of. Last summer he went to the scene of an altercation and a guy who wasn't even the suspect hit him in the back of the head with a five-foot tow chain. Could have killed him! Left him paralyzed! That guy got thirty days in the county jail. Then last week a guy gets caught stealing a screwdriver from Maple Hill Mall, and they give him four years. Cody can't understand how his life can be worth one one-hundredth of a screwdriver.

Where Howard Iris Gardens used to be, up by K-Mart, Cody spots another missing headlight. Big Pontiac. He pulls it over. As soon as it comes to a stop, the door flies open and a slender young woman wearing a long skirt and a sweater steps out into the freezing wind and walks toward car 633 on Millham Drive, her skirt lifting and blowing.

She looks threatening, accusing.

She looks like an angel of God.

"What have I done?" she demands.

"You have a headlight out," Cody says, stiff-faced, getting out. "May I see your driver's license?"

"I do? I didn't know that. I can't afford a new headlight." She stares at Cody.

"Maybe you don't need one. Maybe you just have a short, and it needs to be wiggled a little." Cody walks to the front of her car, opens the hood, and rattles the blind headlight with the heel of his hand. Nothing.

"Nope. Sorry. Guess not," he says.

He takes her license to the car, fills out a ticket, and when he gives it to her, the woman is crying. Cody gets back in his car and waits for her to pull into traffic.

Cody would bet that woman just got over a divorce. She didn't look too good.

He pulls into the procession of cars. Boy, the tears were just streaming down her face when I gave her that ticket, Cody thinks.

He cannot imagine just getting over a divorce and having some guy hand him a ticket like that.

He passes a Honda stalled at an intersection, calls it in, and whips

633 around the intersection, fishtailing snow. His lights are on again; he gets out, stern. The driver, a student in a short sleeved shirt, says the car won't start, so Cody tells him to steer while he goes to the back and pushes. He pushes the Honda out of the intersection and halfway down the block. The wind comes up, and it is cold.

As Cody is driving the kid to the Shell station in the warm car, dispatch sends him a call to assist at the scene of an illegal entry.

Cody drops the kid off at the station and tells him, "Buy a coat." He heads over to the houses by the river, location of the illegal entry call. Bright red, blue, green, yellow, and white Christmas tree lights hang blowing from the front porch of the house. Cody goes inside. The family is sitting in front of the television eating Domino's and drinking Coke. Star Trek is on, with all its weird clarinet music and gongs. Three kids are dangling slices of pizza over their open mouths. Cody's stomach creaks like a house in the wind, then groans. He would like to reach down and grab a slice of pizza right from the box. The mother's watching him from her Laz-y-boy. "She just walked right in. Without knocking. I told her never to do that. She just walked right in. She wouldn't leave." The kids are looking up.

She gives Cody the intuder's address, twice. It's over by the paper mill. "You go over there." He asks for a description. "About two hundred pounds," the woman says, like an accusation, her husband quiet in a chair by the TV, a cup of Coke on his knee. Cody asks the color of the suspect's hair.

"Black," say all three children in unison.

At the suspect's home, a slanting house with a sagging porch and massive icicles stuck down the length of its side, another Public Safety Officer—a new recruit—has arrived at the scene.

The guy's a fireman. Cody stays in the street. The woman steps out her door, turning back and yelling at a gawking boy inside. "Keep it shut." The door closes. She's big. She has black hair.

"What's your name?" the officer asks her. He shines his flashlight in her face.

"Ellen."

"Got a last name?"

"Haynes."

"Did you enter a home at 745 Wheaton Avenue about a half hour ago?"

"Yeah I did and I went in to get my daughter."

"I got news for you," the recruit tells her. "You broke the law."

"No I didn't," says the woman, the hint of a shriek in her voice. "You trying to tell me I can't go get my little girl? When they got her even after I told them she wasn't allowed at their house? Oh, no," she says, "I know my rights."

"All the same, you broke the law," the officer says, his hair shiny with Vitalis. "You tell your daughter not to go in there, or you call us to get her, but you don't just walk in." He folds his arms and stares at her. Cody is standing in the street. "You remember that." The recruit turns to leave. The woman's staring at him.

"You can't tell me that," she yells, following him out in the freezing air as he walks to his car. "I know my rights. I didn't do nothing. I can get her if I want to. You go talk to them."

The door of the house opens, and four kids look out the crack. "Get back in there!" she screams and the door shuts. The recruit starts his car. Cody hasn't said anything to anyone. "I'm sorry this happened," he tells the woman standing on the sidewalk in her bathrobe and slippers.

Cody gets in his car. He thinks, that guy could have listened to her. He could have listened to how important it is for her to have her little girl. He could have said he'd help her get her little girl any time it happened again. Then he could have told her she can't go in somebody else's place without permission. A chimpanzee could have done better a better job than that guy. Now everybody's mad.

He parks behind the defunct auto detailing shop. He's going to monitor traffic at the busy intersection, but instead of watching cars, he just stares at the engine block from a V-8 freezing against the back of the building.

McPeters, Williams, Casey—quit. McClure shot himself; Clark, he knifed up his wife over it. He's going to Jackson, poor devil.

A breadstick turns to paste in Cody's mouth.

This merger is bad.

The headlights and snowflakes go stretching down the road.

If you complain about it, they just tell you anything new takes time to get used to.

A car turns through the intersection, kicks up a chrome wheel trim ring, stabbing a reflection into the night.

Cody is starving.

And he's so lonely he can hardly believe he is sitting there.

THE HOUSES ON CODY'S pot-holed street are wooden. They huddle together on the block with their one-car garages and tricycles frozen into their lawns. From his neighborhood on the hill, Cody can see the lights of the city sunk below him in the darkness of the valley. They shimmer down there, embedded, frail as the lights of the weird glowing creatures at the bottom of the sea.

Cody lives in the cheap part of town. But he's happy with his job, in spite of the pay.

He sits at the dinette with his belt undone, his feet throbbing as he waits for some tuna casserole to heat, when he notices Jan's wearing that Jean Nate` stuff that makes his heart beat hard. His mouth starts watering. She has thick fingers but her skin is smooth. She is like a brook. How he loves her. He hopes she knows how much he does. She must know. She's his honeybun, she's his sweet potato pie. He's told her that before.

Peter appears at the kitchen door, his red hair frowzy as a cloud.

"Wanna play Chinese checkers, Dad?" His eyes are half open. He wavers where he stands, grabs the back of a chair. His eyes close.

Cody pulls him over and hugs him. The house is filled with the good smells of home-cooked broccoli and fried chicken. The kids' plates are stacked on the dinette. Cody's glad to be able to feed his kids! He only wishes he could watch them eat.

Jan turns from filling the sink. "You get back to bed," she says.

"Dad?"

"I can't right now," says Cody. "Sit at the table for a while."

He looks at Jan. She says nothing.

Peter climbs in the chair and watches his father eat. He tells his father what he did today: he made a kite. Jan starts the dishes. Cody can feel the shape of her back with her shoulders arching down.

She's such a box of chocolates.

Cody's gotten good at this job, but the police job is a team effort. Somebody has to be there with dinner ready, and she is. But life, life outside of the job, is always on hold. There's no time except to sleep and eat.

They're learning to cope. They're stronger because of it! They can deal with missing birthdays and holidays. Every year they just about make it.

"What did you do tonight?" Peter asks.

"I said get to bed," Jan finally says.

Cody and his wife look at each other in the tiny kitchen. He does love her, and he always will, though he is not sure what difference that makes anymore. He wants it to be the only thing that matters.

"I'll take him." They climb the stairs to the boys' room. Kyle is tangled in his blankets, sleeping across the room. Peter rolls into bed. Cody kisses his cheek. Peter is warm in his little pajamas. He smells like a kid. He is alive.

In his bedroom Cody can't remember where he hid his quick-release holster. It isn't in the bottom drawer. Jan doesn't like police stuff in the bedroom. A wife can support a husband who deals with other people's problems all day, but she can hinder it, too. He finds it in his old hunting boots. He's not supposed to have it. He's supposed to use regulation.

Cody switches holsters, the stretched holes on his belt showing where his waist used to be smaller. Well, he just ate. Your stomach's bigger. He feels good, carrots and peas and tuna casserole, and he likes having the new holster on. His pistol slides into it smoothly. If Cody lived in England he'd be called a Bobby and he wouldn't have a gun! He'd have eaten fish and chips, whatever those are!

He steps into the bathroom, flushes the toilet, and goes back down. She has been crying. The air in the kitchen drains out between them. He is kissing her, a dry kiss, holding her, when his portable radio goes off, ordering him to investigate a complaint of excessive noise, a barking dog.

CODY PULLS UP UNDER A STREETLIGHT in a neighborhood of split-levels, shuts off the motor, opens a window, and waits. Dispatch says the dog has been barking all night. The caller suspects it's locked in a yard without shelter. The street reminds Cody of a night scene in a movie about London, with its pockets of light in the snow. He's been in one out of every twenty houses in this town, in some of them thirty times.

Presently, there it is. The exasperated yap-yap-yapping of a dog somewhere in the darkness of all those backyards. Cody gets out and heads toward the noise, holding his machined-aluminum flashlight like a spear in his left hand, the right free for his gun. The house appears completely closed up: no footprints, no lights, no tracks. The dog is in a fenced-in yard behind. Cody looks over the fence. The dog, a mutt, shoots to the opposite side of the yard and starts barking.

Wonder why he went over there, Cody thinks. You'd think he'd feel more secure by the house. He goes back up front, stopping to look through the garage windows on the way, and rings the door bell. He bangs on the screen door with the butt of his flashlight. No response.

Cody walks back around to the other side of the yard, and the dog shoots to the opposite side again, barking. Its tracks edge the perimeter of the fence. Cody wants to see whether it has shelter.

The back corner looks like the lowest spot in the fence, and a small tree there provides some limbs to hang onto while Cody climbs over. His belt, its nightstick, revolver, handcuffs, and myriad tools and cases could get hung up on the wire so he has to climb until he is standing on top of the fence like a tightrope, and jump straight down. The dog bursts into a new frenzy when Cody drops into the yard.

All it takes is some old lady with her husband's shotgun. Cody heads toward the shadows of the house. He opens a door open for the dog at the back of the garage, a place for it to stay. He climbs back over the fence.

The street is quiet, now. Under the dome light, Cody looks for the appropriate paperwork from his pile of forms. They'd have sent the Animal Warden if this were daytime. The plain truth is, Cody's not a cop anymore. He's a Public Safety Officer. Not only does he get to be a fireman, he's a dog catcher.

He sits slinging the words into the slots on the form, barely legible. Who cares you can't read it. He's lucky if two of every hundred calls he makes will wind up with an offender going to court.

Once they're there, four of every five of them will be acquitted.

The radio pops. Armed robbery at the Mr. Steak on Portage. Shots fired, suspects heading north, toward town. The vehicle, a tan pickup, is spotted again as it enters patrol area one.

Downtown. Cody listens for the capture, but no transmission is heard.

Tears sting his eyes. Cody's kids won't grow up to be Americans. They'll either be Koreans, or Red Chinese, or we won't be here at all. We live in the most free society in the existence of the world. Even the criminals believe the goofy stuff. Even the people that started it in the first place thought less government was good government.

But it's just an experiment. It's too hard to maintain.

Cody's nostrils ache. Please, God. Help us. We're just living in an illusion of safety. Forgive us, Lord. We're destroying the criminal justice system. The downfall is coming, Lord, and everybody thinks it's because of the economy, or too much population, or wasting natural resources! Oh come on! We're living on the morality of our forefathers, and it is rapidly declining. We're honing justice finer and finer all the time. We're just living on the survival edge!

The dog barks; Cody's guts twist like there's a jack handle in there. Every time he sees a kid with his mom, their last names don't match. Divorce is way up. He visits more couples who are living together than are married anymore. We're screwing up. Save us.

The dog's quiet again.

Cody's fingers loosen his belt.

The radio transmits. The suspects from the robbery have driven through town, up onto campus, and have run the truck up a ditch. Campus scored it. The Campus Police were first on the scene!

Cody draws a breath of the miracle air surrounding this world. It is cool and sweet. He shoves the clipboard onto the seat, rubs his palms together, and heads to the scene. Hallelujah. Campus isn't part of his area, but he's gonna have a look.

HOLY COW. THE TRUCK is sticking straight up out of a bramble ditch next to the Submarine Sandwich Shop with its back wheels in the air. Three cop cars have their spotlights aimed onto it, pinning it into the gully in the crystal night air. It looks bigger than itself, rear end lifting up into the air.

It's beautiful.

The suspects have fled on foot, probably into the dorms.

Criminals, a good place to hide.

Never a dull moment! It's cold as bullets outside, the winter night frozen, locked up like a jail, but the inside of 633 is toasty. The snow falls gracefully and swirls around it as Cody heads back to patrol Area Six.

It's nice and late. It's getting way past midnight. This is when the hunting starts getting good. This is when the creeps start coming out from under the rocks.

A girl waves, frantic, a silhouette in the fluorescent glare from the Seven-Eleven. Cody hits the beacons and pulls into the lot.

"Can you get my keys out of my car?" She crouches in the cold. "I locked them in."

Cody deliberates. "We used to carry something that would let us open locked car doors, but we were sued for damaging people's cars, so we stopped carrying them." The girl is crestfallen. She says nothing; she shivers. "But," says Cody, "I keep one just the same." She is ecstatic. Shoving aside his firefighting gear, he takes his jimmy from the trunk.

Snowflakes blow off the Seven-Eleven around them in the lot. Cody slips it down against the window, into the door on her driver's side, and pops her lock.

Her knees bend. "Thank you."

"No problem." Cody slaps the jimmy against his palm.

633's warm. He cruises, late-night traffic burning tracers across his vision. C'mon, he thinks. C'mon creeps. Cody's ready for some action and a little mayhem. He issues two tickets for missing tail lights, one for no rearview mirror, and one for an illegal turn.

As Cody approaches an intersection, he slows; a late 1970's Monte Carlo is coming down a side street so fast it's going to run the stop. Ten feet in front of the sign all four wheels lock and it skids sideways and stops. Cody pulls to the curb and watches.

The car sits at the intersection for twenty seconds.

"Drinking?" asks Cody. The Monte Carlo spins its wheels pulling out of the stop and accelerates, its exhausts roaring as it takes the curve and heads up Westmain hill.

He's getting on it again! Cody hits the lights and pulls from the side of the road calling in a pursuit to dispatch.

The guy's in a big hurry about something. Too big. By the time Cody gets around the curve at the bottom of the hill the Monte Carlo is halfway to the top.

Cody straightens his leg against the gas pedal. Ahead, the Monte Carlo is passing on the right—and on the left and again on the right as it swerves through the traffic plodding up the hill. 633's motor howls in passing gear, its revolving lights flashing against the sides of cars on the hill as Cody passes.

At the top, Cody catches up to the car and runs within three lengths of its rear bumper, both cars hovering, floating, doing sixty through the residential area, the back of the suspect's car and the trees and houses on the sides of the street pulsing with the flashes of electric blue light from Cody's beacon.

Suddenly the Monte Carlo jumps ahead, its mufflers roaring. Cody calls in the need for assistance and accelerates down Westmain. 633's engine sings and Cody feels the car almost lifting like a jet on the runway, taking off.

Both cars are doing eighty-five and gaining. Like a speeded-up movie, the Monte Carlo shoots awkwardly over the centerline, then just as suddenly, swerves back, across both lanes on the right side, turns abruptly down a side street, and stops.

Cody's right on him and gets out of the car before the guy's brake lights go off. This guy could be some dope-head or felony parole violator. Cody rests his hand on his pistol.

The driver shows Cody his license and an identification card that says he's with the City of Portage: Volunteer Fireman. He's twenty years old, a kid, very polite, saying "Yes, sir," looking up seriously through black bangs hanging into his face.

"I'm on the way to a call." His breath and the inside of his car smell like alcohol.

Cody takes the license, calls it in, asks for verification of the Portage fire call. He sits in 633 wanting to know. Dispatch can't say; Portage will not verify either way.

Cody asks the driver to step out of his car.

The young man's eyes are glassy. "I have reason to believe you've been drinking tonight. I'd like you to walk heel-to-toe along this line," Cody tells him, indicating an imaginary line in the pavement with a wave of his hand.

The kid succeeds neatly for almost ten feet, then loses his balance and takes a step back.

"Pick a number between twelve and fourteen," says Cody. The kid's confused for a few seconds. "Fourteen."

"Put your feet together and press your hands to your side. Tip your head back."

He does. "Shut your eyes. I want you to hold that for, oh, twenty seconds."

He wavers but does not lose his balance.

Two other police cars arrive, parking diagonally across the street. The drivers get out and ask if Cody needs help. He shakes his head no. They direct traffic around the pulled-over Monte Carlo.

"My friend, it is my opinion that you've had too much to drink to be driving tonight."

"Okay," says the young man.

"I want you to bring your hand behind your back," says Cody, and when the young man complies, Cody snaps a handcuff around it.

"Now the other."

Cody seats the kid in the back of 633 and heads to the police station downtown. Dispatch still can't verify the kid's story.

"I'm supposed to report to man the station," the kid says from the back.

"I went to a soccer game at Wing's Stadium with some friends and we had a couple beers. We went to Big Daddy's and had a few more. Then my beeper went off."

Cody listens.

"Can't you take these cuffs off?" the kid asks.

"I'm sorry, but I'm required to leave those on you."

"I feel like a criminal."

"My friend, I'm going to treat you just like my brother," says Cody. "You are being a perfect gentleman, and I appreciate that. But we're going to see if you've had too much to drink."

Whitey says, "What'd you get? A drunk?" and Cody shrugs, smiling. The jail is dismal, dirty, as they walk to the back, past cells, young men lying on long vinyl pads, gray blankets wrapped around their heads to cover their eyes from the light. The walls are stomach-ache green. Stainless steel sinks and pottys stick out of the walls like the toilet on a bus. An old man with a look of terror on his face lifts his head.

"In here."

A messy finger print machine squats on a shelf next to a gray sink. As the kid blows into the plastic tube of the blood-alcohol analyzer, Whitey operates the dials and reads the meter.

"What's it say?" the kid says the second Whitey tells him he can stop blowing. His words run together slightly.

"Well, we won't know what you got until we do the second test," Whitey tells him.

"Yeah but what was that one?" the kid asks again.

Whitey readies the machine for another test. "Okay," he says, "Blow."

The kid blows.

"Harder," says Whitey, watching the meter.

He blows harder.

"Okay, stop," Whitey says.

"What'd I get?" the kid asks, right away.

"Hang on," Whitey answers. "Why don't you sit down." He advances a paper tape from the analyzer and rips it off like the receipt from a cash register, fills out a form, then stands and looks at the kid. "You show a blood-alcohol level of point twelve on the first test and a level of point twelve on the second test," he says and gives Cody the test results for his paperwork.

"Oh God." The young man sinks into his chair, suddenly drained, depressed. He knows he's going to have to stay in jail.

Cody selects the appropriate forms. He reads the man his Miranda rights and informs him he's under arrest. He asks some questions and writes down the answers. The young man is employed as a volunteer firefighter with the city of Portage and as a security guard at Wing's Stadium. He's a high school graduate. He's done a few semesters at the community college in Law Enforcement.

He is studying to be a cop. As he answers, he sounds like he is about to cry. He stares into the center of the room.

"Who do we contact in case of emergency?" asks Cody as he scoops the man's pocket paraphernalia and belt into an envelope.

"Nobody," the kid says.

"C'mon. Let's say you die tonight. Who do we call?"

"Call the morgue."

"Look, you don't have to make this so bad. You're just going to get sober. Maybe you can learn from this experience. Has it ever occurred to you that you may be alcoholic?"

"Of course," says the kid.

"Maybe you'll learn from this, and never be back here. This might be an important day for you."

Whitey takes the kid's prints, rolls his fingers in ink, rolls them again on the spaces of the form. He photographs him.

They lead him to a cell, where he slumps down on the vinyl mat.

There is a stack of magazines and newspapers in the corner.

"Let us know if you want us to light your cigarettes," Cody says.

"Grab a couple of those blankets," says Whitey. "Get some sleep. You'll feel better."

"My career," the kid says.

Cody and Whitey walk down the hall. "He can't be a cop," says Whitey. "Want some coffee? We got some coffee cake."

"No thanks. Just a minute." Cody returns to the kid's cell. "I'm not supposed to do this, and I'm not promising, but I'll try to give you a ride to your car in the morning."

633'S TIRES CRUNCH AND POP over frozen mud tracks. Cody shuts off the motor and the lights. He can barely see the big houses. He's deep back in the development under construction off Raney Road. He's the only car back there. He turns the radio down as low as it will go. He just sits there for a minute.

In the glow of the radio's control panel, he logs tonight's shift in his memo booklet. Slashes for the missing headlights, two circles for the illegal turns, an "S" for the subpoena, x's, dots, and squares for the assists and complaints, a star for the DUI.

Good for him. Good job, Cody. Every real cop in the Department has a reputation for something; Cody brings in drunk drivers. Most cops manage five or ten a year. Cody's record is forty-two.

The radio whispers a far away sound. He turns it off, something he's not supposed to do, something he's never done before.

No sound. A sort of gushing in his ears.

Drunks are exercises in futility. Cases are thrown out over technicalities, defendants acquitted by sensitive juries, juries afraid to accept responsibility for somebody's punishment. They think driving is a right, not a privilege. Any offender can always plea bargain the minimum charge and get his license back.

Cody knows drivers that have six impaired-driving convictions, and they're still driving. Oh, brother.

It's dark out, then Cody sees in the starlight, a ghost town, empty houses, a neighborhood sprawling across a hill before him, fancy, unfinished homes missing all their families. When Cody was a kid he watched Rio Lobo on TV, sitting in the living room with his father. He remembers drinking 7-Up from Dixie cups and eating popcorn from a big wooden salad bowl. He can almost taste the butter and the crunchy warm popcorn in his mouth.

The car is dull with cold. It's as cold as a meat locker. Ferns of frost edge the windshield. Cody's breath goes out ghostly in the dull air before him, freezes, and falls. The cold burns his sinuses, and he is hungry.

When he reaches for the keys, his heart seems to have disappeared from his chest. Cody used to have to drive junkers all the time, he never knew whether they would start. What if the car does not start? How will Cody explain being in the development? What will he say?

It starts. He grabs the shifter. He can't drop it into drive.

Cody cannot continue to eat so much. He must stop this. He wants some coffee and doughnuts big-time, but they are killing him. He has earned some coffee and doughnuts, but he must not have them any more.

He will go to the Dragon Inn and have a pot of tea.

But the Dragon Inn is closed, and at the bright, pink Dunkin Donuts, the girl smiles. Cody orders a large coffee with double cream and sugars, two honey dipped, one maple dipped, and a raspberry filled. He takes the polka-dotted bag to the station downtown to do his paperwork in the break room. His eyes tire as he fills out his forms. He's weary. His hand cramps; it goes numb. The speaker on the wall blows dispatch's static, a continuous sound of frying bacon. These twelve-hour shifts are killing him. It's five o'clock when he finishes, the whole station sleepy with the quietness of night. Cody goes to the front desk to talk to Kate in dispatch. She used to patrol, herself, until a suspect took her gun away from her and cuffed her to the bumper of her own car.

"Hi, Cam." She wears her complete uniform, her badge and Pistol Expert pin, even though she only sits in the dim fluorescent desk light all night anymore. Next to her, Renetta looks comfortable in her sweatshirt.

"Did your volunteer fireman turn out to be driving under the influence?"

"Yeah," says Cody. "Point twelve. He's in the cell right now."

He points above them.

"Good," Kate says. "Those drunks better watch out for you."

She smiles. Cody feels funny. He wants to tell her something, but what can he say? He kind of wishes the kid wasn't up there lying on a mattress. "Thanks," he says. "He was a just a kid partying. I'm thinking about giving him a ride to his car in the morning."

"That'd be nice, Cam. You ought to do that."

They talk about her bowling league, then her face goes slack as she listens to her earphone. She looks at him. "Burglar alarm at Video World. Gorham Street."

Cody drives to the stripmall, wondering who the last remaining Beatle will be. Probably Ringo. He wonders if he will see a body at Video World. He might see a body. The parking lot is empty and cold. The front door's locked tight, its doorknob cold. Cody goes around to the back. The back door could be open. It's possible there could be a body. Maybe he'll go inside. He'll take his pistol out. He's never found a body. He's never fired his gun at anything except practice targets. But the back door is locked tight, there are no footprints in the snow. It's five thirty in Area Six. False alarm, another form.

Cody drives aimlessly through the emerging morning and as the sky glows he can almost hear it, musical. It has a flavor, like glass. It's the light of day! It's a miracle of God! Cody can feel the weight of his eyes in his face. 633's covered almost two hundred miles tonight so far. At six, Kate's voice comes through the radio speaker, reminding Cody to give the young man a ride.

SUN BRIGHTENS A WHITE winter morning. The young man has had some sleep, and he looks better, but he acts sad. He rides silently in the front seat. "Hey, you got out," Cody tells him.

"I'm going to have to turn in all my firefighting gear," he tells Cody.

"Maybe."

The kid is silent again.

His car windows are frosted opaque when they get there, the car a dull green lump in the road, surrounded by frosted lawns. He gets out and slams 633's door. Cody sits waiting to hear if his car will start.

Tired. Cody will drive to the station, where Jan will pick him up, drive him home. They'll fry eggs, hashbrowns, he'll see the boys. Then he'll go to bed, sleep all day, and get up, eat, talk to Jan, and go to briefing to head out on patrol again tonight.

"Officer Cody?" the kid is saying. "Hey Cody. Let me show you this."

Cody breathes. His seatbelt whines, snaking into its retainer. He gets out and walks to where the kid is, crouching over his trunk, working the lock.

With a pop the trunk rises and the kid reaches in and swings out something long, brown, and heavy. He pokes it toward Cody's chest.

Oh. Cody recognizes the little brass ring on the breech. It's a Winchester Model 94 deer rifle.

The kid's looking upset, perturbed. He's looking pretty pissed off. When Cody was in first grade, he saw a wolf cub in a cardboard box, only a few weeks old, grey as ashes, and it was fierce and ugly.

"You wrecked my career, man," the kid says, shucking the bolt like The Rifleman.

Ah well, it's a shame Colonel Sanders doesn't open at seven in the morning. A bucket of Kentucky Fried would be great. It's always wonderful to eat as much as you can when you get it, straight from the bucket, and to save the rest in the refrigerator, and have it later, cold. Kentucky Fried Chickens ought to stay open around the clock.

There ought to be a law.

But then, maybe it doesn't matter.

The kid is sighting down the rifle, aiming the barrel at Cody's heart. His voice goes high with the anguish of betrayal: "You ruined my life." His face twists into a knot.

"No, I didn't." Cody is shaking his head.

A firework blossom of blood imprints the snow as Cody fires his pistol and the kid sits down in the road.

• IT'S SATURDAY •

SKYLINER

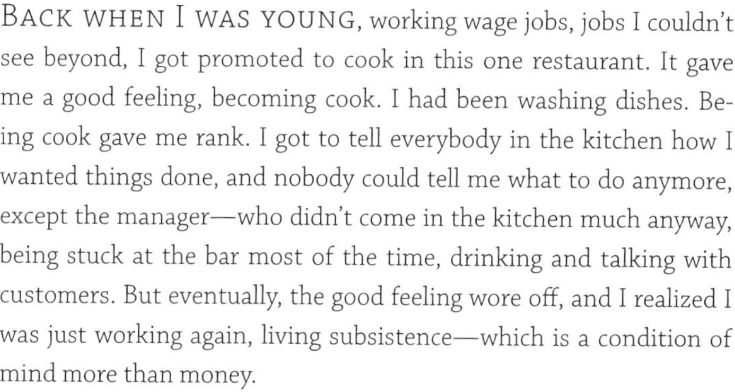

BACK WHEN I WAS YOUNG, working wage jobs, jobs I couldn't see beyond, I got promoted to cook in this one restaurant. It gave me a good feeling, becoming cook. I had been washing dishes. Being cook gave me rank. I got to tell everybody in the kitchen how I wanted things done, and nobody could tell me what to do anymore, except the manager—who didn't come in the kitchen much anyway, being stuck at the bar most of the time, drinking and talking with customers. But eventually, the good feeling wore off, and I realized I was just working again, living subsistence—which is a condition of mind more than money.

I cooked the breakfast shift. Every morning while it was still dark out, I unlocked the place, my breath misty, stars in the sky, maybe one car out front pushing its headlights along. I'd walk into the hot, quiet kitchen, shut off the burglar alarm, turn up the Muzak, then I'd light the stoves, start up the toasters, and turn on the heatlamps. I'd stock up the line. I'd set the lights in the dining rooms, and when the waitresses arrived, all sleepy-faced and bleary, they started the urns of coffee, and we opened up. I cooked breakfasts—eggs, hashbrowns, pancakes, and toast—blending into lunch—Ruebens, Clubs, and fries—for hundreds and hundreds of customers.

At the restaurant, people got along. When the place was busy, it was a team effort, and there was a satisfaction in making it all work right, whole orders coming up at once, plates steaming hot and garnished, the waitresses taking them out right away, new orders coming in all the while, and nobody stopping to slow down. It was like clockwork, when it was happening right.

But most of the time the restaurant was boring. Wipe, stack, weigh out portions into Baggies. Clean a freezer. People would ask for raises because there wasn't anything else to ask for, and besides, they gave them to you—a nickel. When I made cook they bumped me a dime an hour. So what? That was four more dollars a week. I mean, I was barely making minimum wage. Say it had been a dollar . . . just more cigarettes and booze.

But I reconciled myself to the situation. I was living with my brother at the time. He had let me move in after things with my girlfriend went sour. I was lucky for that, and I had a job. I didn't complain. I worked. Each Friday afternoon, I cashed my paycheck and gave my brother some money, then I took what was left and went bar-hopping until the bars closed or I couldn't drink anymore, and drove home. When I woke the next morning, I'd clean out my pockets, and if I found anything, I stuffed it in a toy ukulele I kept in a cardboard box full of clothes.

I got good at that job, you might say, being dependable, and on time, doing inventory, and cooking, the days and weeks and months going by. I made pancake men when the waitresses told me there were kids out there, and sometimes the manager would have me cover for dishwashers who were sick, or fill in for the night cooks, jobs I did even though I knew I shouldn't have to.

One Saturday morning, when I couldn't fit any more money in that ukulele, I stomped on it, and counted what was in it, almost seven hundred dollars. Fives, tens, twenties—seven hundred dollars that, all things considered, I had no use for. What good was it to me? It got to bothering me, that cash. It was supposed to be doing something for me, making everything seem right, but everything was not right. I got to feeling downright rotten over it. It was easy to see that nothing had changed, and the more I thought about it, the more I got to wishing I didn't have that money at all. I had the bills stacked and folded over, jammed down in the toe of a shoe, and when I took that wad out and looked at it, it just seemed greasy.

I WAS LYING AWAKE ONE NIGHT, feeling bad about it, worrying and trying to fall asleep, when I realized that my problem all along had been a matter of attitude. The answer was simple. I just had to spend it, was all, one big lump, on something I had always wanted, something I wouldn't have been able to own if I hadn't made it this far. It would be like getting a prize, like I won something good.

I was relieved, and I fell asleep, but the next morning, I got the creeps again, because I didn't know what the hell my prize should be. Down payment on a Harley? Trip to Vegas? New boots, hat, and a long leather coat?

I thought about it for days. Then, driving home from the restaurant one sunny afternoon, I got a clear feeling. I realized that what I had always wanted was a vintage automobile—a better word would be classic. I wanted a classic car, a big car from the Fifties, a big convertible with fins. I was willing to pay for it. I had the bucks.

I STARTED SEARCHING THE CLASSIFIEDS, hoping for:

> *1957 Chevrolet Convertible, excellent cond.*
> *12,000 miles. Original upholstery. Stored*
> *winters. Must sell. $500. Bob 455-8798.*

or

1954 Mercury Fleetwood. Original paint, chrome. New tires. Runs great. Going into army. $600, offer. 765-0985 after 7:00, keep trying.

But I was lucky even to come across:

1962 Ford Falcon. Runs. Needs windshield, tires. Restore or parts. Rust. See to appreciate. $750. 398-8763 ask for Tony.

No way was I going repair, let alone restore, this thing. My brother had the heating ducts to my room turned off—I couldn't be tearing cars apart in his driveway. Even if it was my own place, and I had the money, I wouldn't have wanted to spend my time fixing a car. No, it would have to run great and look fantastic from the word go.

My brother, his wife, and I were having peas and macaroni and cheese when I was going through the paper and I saw the ad:

1962 Ford Retractible. Good condition. Runs. Stored. $700 987-9863.

"HEE HAW" WAS ON TV, Buck Owens wearing a pair of bib overalls backwards and playing a red, white, and blue guitar. I went into the kitchen and called the number. I asked was the Ford sold.

"Nope, still got it," the guy said.

"What's a retractible?"

"What's a retractible? That's a power hardtop convertible. A hard-top that goes into the trunk."

As soon as he said that, I remembered, as a kid, standing on a curb with some friends one hot afternoon while somebody's uncle pressed a button in his car and the trunk opened, slowly, hinged at the back, and the roof and rear window lifted right off the car's body, separating from each other while they lifted, and then, metal and glass overlapping nice and neat, folded backwards, smooth, into the trunk.

"Oh, wow," I said. "Yeah. I remember those."

"They only made four thousand."

"And it all works?" I asked.

"Works fine," he said.

"Ought to be worth more than seven hundred, then."

"Getting rid of it," he said. "What something's worth isn't always what you can get for it," he told me, and I knew the truth of this statement.

"Where are you?" I asked.

"Okay. You know where the Long Lake Roller Rink is?"

I'd been by it before, in another township. "Yeah."

"Right there," he said. "Go to the ticket booth and tell them you came to look at the car."

IT WAS IN A STORAGE SPACE below the rink. We had to yell, all those skaters up there, Saturday night. The guy got in and started the motor, then held a switch on the dashboard until the roof went in the trunk, kind of jerky. I watched him talk it along. But it did go down. It was still a sight.

"Nice," I yelled.

"All hydraulic," he yelled, sweeping his hand to the end of the car like somebody in a commercial. The car stretched out under the fluorescent lights nailed to the joists, its paint, turquoise, faded in swirls down to the primer. The guy sat in the car grinning and revving the motor while a couple kids—his, I suppose—ran around down there jumping piles of trash and shooting each other with rubber pop guns that fired ping pong balls.

It had fins, by God, and inside the seats sprawled like couches, everything done up in a soft, two-tone pattern, blue and white, with gold threads running through the fabric. The dash and windshield wrapped all around chrome-trimmed and padded, and a blue-tinted band blended into the glass along the top of the windshield for comfort on sunny days. It was fantastic. The steering wheel, translucent plastic, suspended sparkling metal flakes. The steering column housed a scenic 3-D shifter display under a clear plastic dome that lit up fancy in the dark. The gauges receded, all separate, and glowed like tiny stage sets at night. It was truly marvelous. With an illuminated vanity mirror and cigarette lighters on every arm rest, that car was historical. It was absolutely made for cruising!

I felt I had done the right thing, then. The car made a big hit at the restaurant, which pleased me. It caused a sensation whenever I lowered the top down, and once or twice a week the waitresses would come back to the kitchen and say, "Bobby, they want to see it," meaning they had a bar full of interested people out there, and we would all go out back and I'd start it up and show it off. I did like that car. On my way out at the end of a grimy day, I'd slip into the walk-in cooler and steal a six pack, and then I'd drive around Bloomington, motoring. People would tell me later that they had seen me driving and that they waved, and they'd be mad that I hadn't noticed them. And I'd wish I'd seen them and would have to tell them, "I just don't pay attention when I drive."

In time, some of the waitresses who got off work when I did took to riding with me, and you could feel the excitement build toward the end of the shift. Then they'd change into their blue jeans, and I'd steal more beer, and we'd pile into the car and go put on the miles.

We called it "cruising the gut," and we made an art of it, motoring down the city streets, through the heart of downtown, or cruising out beyond the city limits, sipping beers and smoking reefer after work. Maybe we'd pick up Lenore's kids from school, or we'd run to Marlene's brother's house for a bag of grass, or we might all drive to some little tavern on a highway running away from Bloomington to drink and shoot pool. We got so we knew the back roads, and we had favorite routes which we'd drive with the top down when the weather was good. I put a big, healthy stereo in it, and the sound was mighty in there, it had presence, like the organ in Saint Patrick's Cathedral, and it gave us goosebumps to belt along, nice and high, listening to anybody's choice. We'd drink and drive and put the miles behind us, Merle Haggard or Frank Sinatra singing their hearts out on cassette.

That car rode low. It had dual exhausts that were stock and a big motor, a V-8 that a guy in a gas station told me used to be advertised as having "Neck-Snapping Power." And it was fast. Out in the farming country the road ran straight through the trees for half a mile then ramped over a culvert. We knew nothing finer than to start that Ford an eighth of a mile back and come at that culvert accelerating, all of us pressed back into our seats, the tape player turned up, Frank Sinatra singing "High Hopes," the speedometer bobbing, big Rocket V-8 hammering, roaring, sides of the road smeared, the culvert coming at us like a wall—and then to take that lump in the road with grace, to lift off the ground and fly, ten, twenty, thirty feet, before coming down thrashing, me and that Ford full of waitresses.

"Oh Bobby," those waitresses would say, "Let's go jump that culvert," and we would. We laughed and cheered every time.

NOT ALL THE WAITRESSES came, though. Some didn't want to, especially Monique. "Unique Monique," was how I thought of her. She had sulked around the kitchen since the day she started. She didn't have kids, and she wasn't divorced, or even married. She was in college. She hardly talked to the rest of us, let alone went riding. But one afternoon she stopped me on my way out the back door, stood in front of me and said, "You sure do like to drive around with those girls."

She was angry. So I told her she could come along if she wanted to, and she said she would.

They let her ride up front. Everybody was quiet, at first, smoking cigarettes. But after a while she wondered where everybody lived, so we drove by everybody's place, which she liked, and then she wanted to know where we went on our trips, so we told her about the rock quarries, and drove her to them, and we were headed for Little Bear Dam, when she asked for a beer. When she was done with it, she threw the bottle at a sign and hit it. After that, everybody felt better. When we dropped her off that night she said she'd had fun and asked if she could ride again tomorrow. Everybody said, "Sure."

She started coming every time, and we were glad to have her. She liked riding, listening to the music. She'd hang her head out the window, her hair blowing all around. When I cranked it up to ninety, she'd throw her head back and laugh. "Faster!" she'd say. She spread a general good feeling in the car.

She partied with us and always volunteered at the liquor store. If anybody wanted to go home early, she'd say, "Aw, come on! You better ride up front!" and everybody'd have to climb over the seats until the person who wanted to go home was sitting there, and it would make the difference. We liked her attitude. She was smart. It was Monique who figured out we could go rail riding. We'd straddle the tires over the abandoned railroad tracks that run every whichway out of Bloomington. We'd let the air out of them so they cupped the tops of the tracks, and then we'd ride the rails, across the trestles and through tunnels of overgrowth to whatever little country town they led to. We'd drive slow into town, a car coming into the railroad crossing instead of a train coming down the old railroad tracks, traffic stopped watching us, every one of us laughing and satisfied. Then we'd turn onto the main street, find a gas station, and inflate the tires for the trip back home.

We got to staying out later and later, all of us, and she was always the last one to want to be dropped off. She and I began driving around together after everybody else went home. It got to where we were dropping everybody else off earlier and earlier, then, so we could drive through the state park while the sun was setting, or out to one of the drive-in theaters, just to pay our fares and be together on the big seat. It wasn't long before the group stopped coming at all.

We rode in the evenings and on weekends, sitting side by side as the flat farmlands passed by. We liked to cruise small towns, buying ice cream at their Dairy Queens, wandering their dirt roads. We'd stop in a field, and she'd pick flowers. Then we rode along with a bouquet of chicory in the ashtray. One time, we drove to the amusement park in Michigan City. Another time, Chicago.

She had brown eyes. She was slender, almost skinny, but soft. She could be nervous. Sometimes, when I wanted to hold her, she kind of fidgeted, wiggling around in my arms without really letting go of me; other times, she was still, we both were, and she just poured herself into me.

Her father was a bishop, I found out, in charge of two hundred churches in Pennsylvania. Her mother played a cello in a symphony. They lived in a half million dollar house in Philadelphia. Monique had a sister, and a brother, but she was oldest and special to her parents, who expected a lot from her all the time. When she went home, they gave her curfews. They told her who she could date. She said they grounded her for six weeks one summer because she didn't come home by ten o'clock one night, and that September, wouldn't send her to school in France. They made her stay in Pennsylvania. She had to graduate from a public high school.

She said she had wanted to kill herself that year. She was going to college in Bloomington, and she was staying there during the summer, supporting herself, she said, because she didn't want to go home.

Me, I've been lost in the sandwich between my older brother and younger sister since I can remember, and I've never been to France, and I wouldn't know a five hundred thousand dollar house if it shook my hand. But I liked her a lot, and it bothered me, all she'd been through, because God knows, life can be tough. My father ran a pet shop for a while and was good at it, but he went bankrupt anyway, and then spent a year in the county jail for bouncing checks. That was the year I dropped out of school and started working.

None of it mattered, between us. We had good times. We drove around getting high. We laughed a lot. She liked the car to go fast.

I was staying at her place so much, I moved out of my brother's.

"See you back here in a while," he told me the day I left.

I was loading up my stuff in the back seat.

"Fuck you," I said, not joking. "I'm not coming back here."

I was glad to be leaving, for both our sakes.

Then I told him, "Thanks."

Philosophy was what she studied, and she was going to be a professor. She said she would have a brand new car. She said she would take me to Europe, that she could speak French and German. That fall, when school started, she quit the restaurant and went back to taking classes. I'd go over to her house after work, and make dinner—stir-fried shrimp, broiled red snapper and potatoes, wine—and we'd eat together when she got home. She'd tell me about Europe, the delicious food you could buy hot on the street, the water on the coast of France blue as paint, the churches and the wars they'd had, and she showed me pictures and slides she had. We stayed home together nights, or she took me to movies at the university, old ones, or European ones, ones with subtitles. It was a good feeling to go up on campus and sit in a lecture hall with a bunch of college students. I liked to prop my feet on the chair in front of me and watch the people come in talking, before the lights went down and the movie started. Then we'd all watch. Those movies were beautiful and fascinating to me, even the weird ones. They stayed with me for days.

We didn't ride around so much, though, and instead went to dinner once in a while, or to a movie—but mostly we stayed home. I started reading books—I read *Wired: The Unauthorized Biography of John Belushi* and *Going After Cacciatto*, books I think every American should have to read. She read books by Ayn Rand and Emerson and Friedrich Nietzsche. I wanted to know what they were about, and

I started *Thus Spake Zarathustra*, but it was too goofy for me, and finally, I realized I couldn't finish it.

She was in her head all the time, and she started staying at the library through the evening, or if she did come home, bringing her friends, who would fill up the kitchen and spill out into the living room, drinking beer and shooting the crap about Individualism and The Death of Metaphysics, and I would listen and talk a while, about the weather or baseball, but even that would get complicated, and I would have to go watch TV. At first, it didn't matter, our not being together nights, but in time we stopped even going to movies. So some nights, when she was at the library, I went to the movies alone, and more than once, I found out she was going to them herself, with her friends.

She was making more money than I was, on scholarships alone. One afternoon, on the way home, I stopped at the community college for some brochures. I figured maybe I could go. I was asleep on the couch when she came home that night, late.

She kissed me then went into the kitchen. I heard her open a beer. She came back out and sat down in a big chair across from me.

"What are those for?" she asked. The brochures were on the coffee table.

"Community college. I was thinking about giving it a shot."

"Giving what a shot?"

"Getting some education," I said. "Something like a drafting degree."

She shrugged. "That's stupid," she said. "You don't want a drafting degree."

"Sure I do," I said. "They can place me after two years. Then I could transfer to a four-year program, and get paid while I earn something even better."

She put her beer down. "You don't need community college," she said. "You cook. You're great at it. You like it. Don't worry about money."

"I'm not worried about money," I said. "I just don't want to be a cook forever. I want to do something with my life."

She frowned, bags under her eyes as dark as someone's in a mental institution. "Just relax," she said. "Why can't you let us have fun?"

"That's what I'm trying to do," I told her.

ONE NIGHT A COUPLE WEEKS LATER, we decided to go out. The paper said there was a talent show at the community college, so we went. There was a comedian, a belly dancer, and magician, and the whole show would have been good. But she yawned and sighed and squirmed around in her seat the whole time.

We were driving home, the only sound in the car the whir of the heater fan. It was cool out. We hadn't done much in the Ford in the past weeks, I realized. It had reverted to basic transportation. Even during a patch of Indian summer we'd been through, the top hadn't been down. We hadn't even listened to the radio. It occurred to me, I'd never shown it to her friends. I thought about the car as we drove along. It had been through a lot. I felt bad about it. The car was a collector's item.

"I'm going to get this car painted," I said. "I'm going to get it looking good."

"You're going to get it painted?" she said. "What color?"

"You know," I said. "Stock. Factory color—turquoise. This car's a classic. It needs to be taken care of."

It was quiet and dark in the car. I could feel the wheel bearings and the motor and tires, everything spinning beneath me.

"Pink," she said.

"What?"

"Paint it pink. That's what kind of car this is. They should have painted it pink in the first place."

We drove in silence. The dividing line came and went, flashing and disappearing, spearing through the patch of headlight shining on the road.

"You don't love me," she said.

"Don't say that."

"You don't."

"That's not true."

"Well, it doesn't matter," she said. "I don't love you."

I gripped the wheel. "Oh come on," I said. "We've got a lot for each other."

"No," she said. "I don't want it. I want out. We can be friends. You can stay tonight, but not in my bed. Tomorrow you get your stuff out."

"I'll leave tonight if that's what you want."

She looked out the window. "I don't care. Just get me home."

We were on the highway, going seventy already, but I gunned it. The big V-8 opened up and the exhausts roared. The road speeded up beneath us.

"Slow down," she said.

I straddled the centerline.

"Slow down!" she yelled. I pushed the gas pedal hard, flat to the firewall. We were doing maybe eighty-five. She straightened an arm on the dashboard.

"You bastard!" she yelled, and she reached up and unlatched the roof. Catching air, it jerked back with a bang, and my face hit the steering wheel.

The car had slowed to fifty. I pulled over. Something in my mouth was cut. Blood was seeping into it. I swallowed.

"Get out," I said.

She sat there while I worked the wrecked roof into the trunk as best I could, then we drove to her apartment. I got my clothes and went to drink shots of whiskey at a bar until it closed, then I went to my brother's. I slept in the back seat.

The next day, he helped me put the car up on blocks next to his house. We were going to find a roof for it and fix it ourselves, but it just sat there. It sat there after I found my own place and moved out, and it sat there after my brother sold the place himself and left. The idea was, we were supposed to be able to go back and get it when we wanted. I'd drive past it on my way to school once in a while, and see it sinking, parts missing. Then he called me one morning to say he had been by the place and noticed it was gone.

Sure—I feel bad about it from time to time. Who wouldn't, I'd like to know. A couple weeks ago, me and my wife were helping haul trash from her folks' garage, when we came across a stack of old magazines. The first one I flipped through, here's this full-color, two-page spread for the 1962 Ford Skyliner, complete with a stop-action shot of the roof going into the trunk, and a sharp looking guy and a pretty girl standing by it, smiling to beat the cars. I couldn't believe my eyes. The car in the picture was turquoise!

"Get a load of this," I said to my wife. "They sure knew how to advertise cars back then, didn't they?"

"That thing looks ridiculous," she said. "Who would want to drive such a thing?"

"Are you crazy?" I said. "They built beautiful cars back then. I used to have one of those."

"Dream on," she said.

CAPITOL

BILLY RANG THE DOORBELL and waited for someone to open the door. He was panting. He had kept up with the traffic on Liberty, pumping so hard his feet almost came off the pedals, the bike all springy and dangerous in his hands. On Calley's street he'd jumped the curb and shot across the lawn, still pumping, then locked up the rear wheel at the last minute in a fishtailing skid across the grass and jumped off the bike while it was still moving.

The bike had crashed in the hedge. It lay there now. Billy's feet hurt from having jumped off the moving bike, and his nostrils stung. His bike was in the bushes. It was rugged. He loved it.

Billy couldn't hear anything on the other side of the door. Mr. Calley's big white convertible was not in the driveway, which was good news for Billy. Mr. Calley was funny. He was always smirking at Billy. It wasn't being smirked at that bothered Billy, it was that he didn't understand why Mr. Calley kept doing it. Once, when Billy wanted to know what the hieroglyphics on Mr. Calley's tie meant, Mr. Calley told him they said, "Go soak your head" and gave him one of his smiles.

The door was tall, enameled white, with a cool coat of condensation on it. Billy wanted to draw in the mist on the door with his finger, but he didn't do it.

The door yanked opened, sucking air. "I got a rabbit!" Nile said. He spun around and took off running. Billy stepped in and shut the door and ran down the hall chasing Nile, through the dining room, all the way upstairs to Nile's bedroom.

Nile had his arms in a large cardboard box. He lifted up a big black rabbit like a magician. "His name's Sneakers." The rabbit's black fur glistened. Niles held it under its arms, out with its rear hanging down. It had white paws and a white, fluffy tail. Its nose was going up and down. It held its ears pressed against its back.

Billy petted the rabbit's head. It was smooth, almost slippery. He petted the soft ears. Sneakers was warm all over. Billy could feel his muscles, tight beneath the skin. The fur was shiny and soft. Billy looked down into the box. There was nothing in it but some turds.

"What does he eat?"

Sneakers brought its back feet to Nile's wrists and kicked. Nile lowered Sneakers quickly to the floor. "He wants to go down now. They scratch."

Sneakers stayed on the floor where Niles had set him down. His ears came up, and he took a hop, then another. He took three hops in a row, under the bed.

They lay on the carpet to look at him.

Sneakers moved around among the dust bunnies, dishes, and socks taking tiny hops before coming to a stop in the corner. He gathered his paws beneath him and sat there in a lump. Niles got his Maglite and aimed the beam at him. Sneakers' ears were pink inside, crisscrossed with veins. His eyes glowed red. His nose was going up and down.

"What does he eat?" Billy asked.

"Potatoes," Nile said. "Rabbit chow." Sneakers sat there hunched up. He was frozen. "I'm going to teach him some tricks," Nile said.

Billy wondered what Sneakers was thinking. He pulled his head out from under the bed and sat up. He used to have a cat, Moose. Moose could fetch paper wads. He liked Puss 'n Boots. Moose could hear the can opener no matter where he was and always came running to see what was being opened in case it was for him. He had come to the front door meowing in a storm, and stayed for two years. He slept on Billy's bed and purred when Billy petted him. One day Billy found him stretched out in the yard. He had been hit by a car.

Billy looked around the floor, all covered with M&M's, Hot Wheels cars, Payday and popsicle wrappers, balled-up underwear, and silver CD's. One wall of Nile's room was filled with bookshelves. In it, an aquarium filled with pink light bubbled air as some fish hovered and drifted through the bubbles. One was chasing another back and forth, both of them shooting end to end. On a shelf above the aquarium, on Nile's TV, Yosemite Sam was trying to get into a fort Bugs Bunny wouldn't let him enter.

Nile's wall of bookshelves was full of books, including a 24-volume encyclopedia. Each volume was full of photographs Billy loved to look at.

From a poster on Nile's wall, a blow-up of Humphrey Bogart looked down on them. Humphrey Bogart looked drunk. Billy wondered what was so important about him but felt like a nerd because he didn't know.

Nile had a computer in his room and on the desk, an ant farm with nothing in it, cool-looking with its green barns over the chamber where the ants would go.

"Where'd you get that poster of Humphrey Bogart?"

"He's cool. My dad gave me that. He got it in New York."

Nile's dad brought Nile stuff from his trips all the time. He owned a fishing reel company and was always going somewhere. Once, he gave Nile some silver Mexican spurs.

Billy stood up and clapped his hands. "Hey! Let's build models!" he said. He had four dollars. "Want to go to the Hobby Shop?"

"You scared Sneakers," Nile said from under the bed. He crabbed his way farther underneath. His legs were sticking out, wearing Lee Doubleblacks and a pair of British Knights basketball shoes.

On the mattress lay Nile's electric guitar, a replica of Eddie Van-Halen's, red with stripes going every which way. Billy sat on the bed next to it. The pickup cord ran to a Marshall amp. Nile was taking lessons with a guy who had played on a Kiss record. Niles had a bunk-bed, even though he didn't share his room with anybody.

Billy didn't say anything. He had four dollars and he wanted to buy a model. Nile backed out from the bed with Sneakers clamped between his hands. "Okay," he said. "My Grandma sent me twenty bucks. You can spend the night." He lifted Sneakers over the side of the box and plunked him down.

THEY WENT DOWN TO THE KITCHEN. At the sink, Nile's little brother, Brian, was doing the dishes. Nile's mom stood next to him.

"We're going to ride our bikes down town," Nile told his mother. Brian tipped a plate up out of the suds with a wooden spoon.

"Get your hands in that water," Mrs. Calley told him.

"It' s too hot."

"Wash those dishes," she said, turning on the water and pushing Brian's hands under the suds.

Brian yelled.

"Okay?" Nile said.

Billy almost laughed. That was really funny, Brian yelling likethat.

"That's fine, honey," Nile's mom said.

Billy watched Brian whimpering over the dishes. Nile tapped him on the shoulder. He had a stack of Oreos in each hand. He handed some to Billy. "C'mon." He nodded to the front door.

On the way out of the kitchen, Billy heard Mrs. Calley tell Brian not to leave the sink until all the dishes were done. He heard dishes bonking around in the dishwater.

"What'd Brian do?" he asked when they got outside.

"I don't know." Nile shrugged. "Nothing?"

IT FELT GOOD TO BE BACK ON HIS BIKE. Riding bikes was fun. Nile liked riding too. They hunched over the bars for maximum coasting speed down Westmain hill, gaining speed, coasting too fast to pedal.

At the bottom of the hill, Nile banked into Try's IGA and shot across the parking lot, pumping around the back, past the dumpsters. Then he ducked, cruising underneath a semi trailer. Billy stopped pumping and coasted. Nile had made it through without slowing down, but Billy had been hurt before. He'd seen it coming. He went anyway. He ducked down. Under the trailer, the space between the frame and his handgrips kept getting smaller. He didn't look at them. He was afraid he might tip and get his hands caught.

But he made it.

They cut through the parking lot of the Jetclip factory, around the plant to the path beside the train tracks that went downtown.

It came out by the park. They rode across the pedestrian bridge over the fountain, and down the sidewalks of the outdoor mall, even though the signs told them to get off their bikes and walk.

They locked the bikes to a parking meter in front of Louie's Pipe Shop so they could go inside for candy. The shop smelled so strongly of tobacco that Billy's eyes watered. Billy and Nile went to the glass case and checked out the gum and candy bars while the clerk and a man talked about pipes. They were having a discussion. The clerk got pipes down from the wall out and put them on the counter for the man.

"Let's look at magazines," Billy said. They went to the magazine rack and flipped through issues of Model Railroader. The clerk and the man kept talking about pipes. Billy and Nile walked quietly to the rack in the corner and looked at dirty magazines. The women in one magazine were stretching the necks of their shirts down below their bazongas. Billy giggled.

"Stop," Nile said, looking at the clerk in the mirror above them, but he started giggling too. They put the magazine back and went to the comic book rack, laughing. They looked at superhero comics until the man bought a pipe and left. Then they went to the counter and looked at candy while the clerk put the pipes away. When he finished, they each bought ten sour grape gumballs for a dollar.

"Let's walk," Nile said, outside. "There's a shortcut through Cat's Pajamas." Billy had never been in Cat's Pajamas. It wasn't a kids' store. They went through it anyway, Billy chewing a soggy wad, six gumballs at the same time, his jaws aching. They passed tea kettle whistles, refrigerator magnets shaped like crabs, knives with pigs for handles, hanging mobiles made out of tiny plastic television sets, cookie jars that looked like scared, squawking hens, and cutting boards with spikes on them for holding the meat. Billy decided to buy a yellow tea kettle whistle for his mom on her birthday—they were six dollars—but other than that, he was glad to get to the back door.

It let them out onto a little parking lot with an alley on the other side. Piled with garbage at the backs of restaurants, the alley smelled rotten. Billy couldn't chew his gum. He spit it out and held his breath as they walked through it to Muncie Avenue.

The air was fresh on Muncie, but even though it was only a few blocks from the downtown mall, Muncie was a ghost town. There were tall brick buildings with empty dark windows. Some front windows were covered with plywood. Some were just broken glass. A few had stuff in them—electric fans, bows and arrows, wrenches and trophies lying on the floors of the display windows where mannequins used to be. Signs painted on boards hung over the doors: "Bob's Fan Sales" or "Ted Freer Pro Archery" or "Value City Tool and Trophy." But no cars went by. Nobody was even in the stores.

Nile and Billy passed a marquee that said *Capitol* overhead, all knocked-out like teeth in a cartoon. Plywood covered the front of the building, but in the gaps between the sheets, they could see it was purple and tan, with cement curls and leaves on the corners and around the doors. There was a booth out front, covered with warped, dirty plywood. Billy and Nile pulled a sheet of it. It came off.

Underneath was a glass box with a door in the back. On the slate counter was a paper cup that had come undone at the seams and a curled piece of paper that said "closed" in faded ball-point pen. There was a circle cut in the glass for talking through and a slot for the money and tickets. Billy wanted to get inside.

"This is totally radical," Nile said.

They were under a ceiling of lightbulb sockets. In back, on either side of the booth, were doors. The door on the left side was open a little, chained from the inside, and Billy threw his weight on it. The chain straightened with a crack. They took turns looking inside. There was a lobby in there, and a concession stand draped with fabric, stacks of chairs, an outboard motor, a lawnmower, and boxes—junk, brooms, everything shoved every whichway on powdery red carpet. It smelled like the inside of a busted refrigerator.

The door was open enough for Nile to get his leg in. He turned around with his leg inside and jammed himself in backwards. He had to turn his head and hold his hands over his ears to get inside.

His hand came out. "C'mon," he said.

Billy looked back onto the empty street, then squeezed through.

The room was dark and damp. Light came in sheets from the edges of the doors. The ceiling disappeared into darkness. Powder from the floor clumped to Billy's shoes as he walked around the dark, silent lobby. He felt like he was walking on the moon.

"Maybe there's some candy," Nile whispered.

"It would be too old," Billy whispered back. He lifted a roll of paper from a box and tried to unroll it. It tore like a wet paper towel. It was a poster. It had a horse on it. He put it back.

The concession stand was huge, pushed out round from the back wall, covered with folded red velvet. Mirrors and plaster leaves and flames shot up behind it like roman candles and rockets in a fireworks display. Billy felt along the counter until he found the little door. He turned the knob and went inside. Sacks were piled up behind the counter, leaning, the bottom ones busted open, popcorn kernels all over the floor. Billy scooped up a handful and threw them into the darkness across the room at Nile.

Nile was by a staircase, looking through a box of letters. The popcorn made a machine gun sound against the wall behind him, and he jumped off the floor with both feet in the air and threw his arms out, flinging a letter R away from him like a Frisbee. It sailed all the way across the room and hit the other wall.

"You ass!" Nile whispered on his hands and knees in the darkness. "You scared the shit out of me." He was on his hands and knees. Billy started laughing and coudn't stop. He kept laughing.

"Stop," Nile whispered, but Billy couldn't, thinking of Nile in the air like that. It was so funny, Nile in the air. It was the funniest thing he had ever seen, Nile jumping. He tried to stop, he tried holding his breath, but he burst out laughing harder. He sat on a sack of popcorn and looked at the floor. He took a deep breath, and held it, but started laughing again, right away, laughing so hard his stomach hurt and tears came from his eyes. He felt silly, crying, then scared that he couldn't stop. He wanted to stop. He couldn't.

He had to walk away from the concession stand pinching his nose, looking into the dark ceiling, thinking on purpose of his bike, locked in front of Louie's Pipe Shop, to get his mind off Nile.

He stopped and almost started a few times, before he stopped for good. His mouth tasted salty then. He felt tired, but strong.

"Asshole," Nile whispered and disappeared up the staircase.

Billy followed, running into the darkness. Upstairs, faint light glowed from the staircase at the other end of the long, curving lobby. There were stone benches on the floor, and in the walls, statues of men with leaves around their heads.

"Hello," Nile said to one of them.

They went into the bathrooms. Light from the windows burned their eyes. The girls' bathroom had a separate room with counters in it and mirrors from the floor to the ceiling. The boys' bathroom had mirrors on the walls too. Billy peed into the paint chips at the bottom of one of the urinals.

"Hey," Nile said. He was standing on top of one of the toilets. "Tarzan," he said, and he jumped off, catching the rail over the bathroom door like catching the monkey bars. He hung there, swinging on it.

Billy climbed on the toilet next to Nile's and jumped off too, catching the rail. He could see himself stretched out, hanging in the mirror. He felt a thrill in his guts that moved down, burning and tingling, between his legs.

"Wah-HOO!" he yelled, kicking his legs as fast as he could move them.

"Shut up!" Nile said, clenching his teeth. He dropped and ran out of the bathroom. Billy followed out to the lobby then up the stairs through one of the archways, into the balcony. They came out in a sloping field of seats. The air seemed to go off all around them.

"God," said Billy. They groped down the steps to the railing and stood there. They were in the middle of the theater, surrounded by black space. It seemed to shimmer. Billy stared hard into the darkness, his eyes adjusting, blackness pulsing red. He felt like he was inside the lungs of some enormous, wonderful creature. He could just make out the stage, then the curtains, held back, soft, all around.

"Screen down there," Nile whispered.

"No. . . . Stage."

"Is not," said Nile, but it didn't matter. Standing in the middle of the theater, Billy felt like a diamond, energy inside him proof he would always be fascinated by the world.

"Hey," Nile whispered. Billy turned around and saw faint light coming from the little square of the projection booth.

"Let's go," Billy said. They found the door at the top of the balcony, and up a set of turning stairs behind it, the projection room, where a single light bulb hung, burning, dim, shining on nothing but chunks of crumbled plaster and the bolts on the floor where the projectors used to go, and a dusty wooden chair.

They went down to the balcony, then down the balcony stairs to the lobby. Billy crouched on his way across the floor to the door.

"We didn't see the screen," Nile whispered.

"So what. Let's go."

"No." Nile ran into the theater. Billy followed, down long sloping aisles to the stage. He felt like he was in some kind of goofy cave, red going to black like somebody's insides.

"See?" said Nile. The screen was a couple stories tall, a cement wall painted white.

"Okay," said Billy. Hey, he realized, I was here before. A movie about dead people in a floating house, then going to his father's apartment after it was over, watching Funniest Home Videos while drinking Seven-Up out of colored aluminum tumblers. That's all he remembered about that day. His father was gone now and, standing in the empty theater, it occurred to him there would always be things he would never understand.

"There," Nile said, pointing to a door with a rectangle of light etched around it. They went over to the side of the theater. The door had a board through the handle. Nile slid the board out and dropped it. He pushed the door and looked out the crack.

"Decent," he said. He opened it and they stepped out, into an alley. Two men were standing there. One of them stepped forward, circled their necks with his arms, brought their heads down to his stomach, and banged them together so hard Billy saw a flash of light. Nile started laughing. Billy grabbed the man's wrist and twisted his head against the man's arm trying to get free. The man let go and when they stood he grabbed their necks with his big hands. He squeezed Billy's neck so hard Billy couldn't breathe and pushed both of them up against the wall. He held them there.

"Hell you doing?" the man said. He looked like a baby, with big fat lips, but he was huge.

"Please sir," said Nile. "The door was open." The man twisted the collars of their shirts and pushed his fists into their necks. The back of Billy's head scraped the wall. Something poked his back.

"No." The man looked at Nile. "I said what you doing." He had red hair on his arms.

"We went in to look around," Billy said. "We pushed the door open to get in. We know we weren't supposed to." The other man was quiet, watching. He was thin, with rails of slicked-back hair. He nodded.

"Damn right about that," the big man said, looking at Billy. "What's your names?" he said, looking back at Nile.

"Troy Elliot," Nile said.

"Billy Taylor," Billy said.

The man looked at them. "Well, Troy and Billy," he said, "I guess I won't be calling the cops today and having you taken to jail. So long as you promise you won't ever come back here."

Billy nodded his head yes.

"We promise, sir," Nile said.

"Sure," the man said. He pulled them away from the wall and rammed them against it. He leaned down in their faces and grinned. His teeth were capped, black lines between the white and the gums. "You just a couple of dumb shits, you know that?"

Billy and Nile stood held to the wall.

"Yes, sir," Nile said. "Thank you."

Billy twisted his neck against the man's grasp. He stood on his toes and grabbed his wrist. The man squeezed Billy's neck, then let them both go. "Get out of here!" he yelled.

Nile ran, but Billy walked out of the alley back to Muncie Avenue. They headed toward the Toy and Hobby Shop without saying anything. Billy wanted to relax. His neck hurt.

A few blocks from the theater, while they waited on a corner for the signal to change, Nile said, "Boy that was lucky."

"Heck no," Billy said. "That guy was an ass. It wasn't even his place."

"Yeah but," said Nile. "You told him your name. If he wants he can call your mom now. We could still get in a lot of trouble. That was stupid, what you did."

Billy wanted to tell Nile to shut up. "Hell no he won't call her. He won't do anything. We can go back there anytime we want. I'll go back right now."

"Go ahead," Nile said. The light changed to "walk" and Billy crossed the street. Nile went with him. They walked along without talking.

"So?" said Nile.

"So what?" Billy said.

Nile shrugged.

"STILL WANT TO BUILD MODELS?" Billy said when they got to the Toy and Hobby Shop.

"All right." They went inside and walked past the bicycles, Sesame Street dolls, and gas-powered planes to the back of the store, where the model kits were stacked on three rows of shelves. They took separate rows. Billy looked over models in his row for a while. He picked a P-51 Mustang kit. The box said it had retractable landing gear, a spinning prop, and a sliding canopy. He slit the plastic wrap with his fingernail and looked inside the box. The parts were molded in silver, clear, and black plastic. Good. He wouldn't need paint. He couldn't pay for paint. He spotted the two halves of the teardrop gastank and four halves of bombs for under the wings. Parts he couldn't identify made him want to buy the kit so he could find out what they were. It was seven dollars, though. He had six bucks from taking out the garbage and mowing the lawn, and he had spent a dollar for gum. Plus he needed glue. Maybe Nile would lend him a couple bucks. He took the kit around the aisle.

Nile had a box as big as a suitcase open on the floor. It was the USS Enterprise Aircraft Carrier. He was holding a plastic frame with about fifty tiny jets molded on it.

"I've built that," Nile said looking at Billy's P-51. "I got it for my birthday. The parts don't fit. It's lousy."

Billy thought he would like to try it someday, anyway. He put it back on the shelf.

"This is twenty-seven bucks," Nile said, crouched over the box of gray plastic. He put the lid on and put it back. They looked a while longer. "Hey, I could build this again," Nile said, pulling a Patton tank from a stack of kits. He checked the box over.

"Yeah, it's cool," Billy said. He had built it before, too. Its treads moved, and it had a rotating turret with elevating cannon, and a swiveling machine gun. Billy wanted to choose it himself, but Nile had seen it first. Besides, he couldn't afford it.

"I guess I'll get this," Nile said. He put the top on the box. He looked at Billy.

Billy checked price tags until he spotted a four-dollar-and-seventy-five-cent Bell Cobra helicopter, set up for 'Nam. It had machine guns coming out the doors and cluster rocket launchers on the skids, like the real thing. Inside the box were decals to give it that pulled-back, red mouthful of fangs, like a shark. Plus it was bigger than Billy expected for the money.

"I'll get this," he said. The models were from different wars, but that didn't matter. They would be fun to put together, and when they were finished, Billy could hold his and walk around the room and down the hall, peering through it, spinning the rotor blades with his finger, pretending he was inside flying over real terrain, firing machine guns and dropping bombs.

BACK AT NILE'S HOUSE, they passed through the dining room on their way upstairs.

Billy stopped. Brian was standing in the corner like a statue, his eyes all bleary and dark and hard. Something was on his head. A can of beans.

"Must have been being bad," Nile said.

They looked at Brian.

"What'd you do?" Billy asked, but Brian just stared.

"C'mon," Nile said. They went through the living room. Nile pointed to the phone. "Tell your mom you're spending the night," he said and ran upstairs. Billy didn't like being in the living room alone. He hoped his mother was home. She had been, that morning.

She picked up the phone.

"Mom, I'm at Nile's," Billy said.

"What you doing?"

"Building models. He got a rabbit."

"That's nice."

"Yeah. What are you doing?"

"I'm going to Clyde's tonight, honey," she said.

"Yeah, we went downtown. We're going to make models. Can I spend the night here?"

"Sure, then," said his mom.

"Okay," Billy said. "See you tomorrow."

"Bye, honey."

Out the window, Mr. Calley's Buick was pulling up the driveway. Billy went upstairs.

He got in Nile's room and closed the door. The TV was on. Nile was sitting on the floor with his model in front of him, running the dial with the remote. Sneakers was in the middle of the floor. News was on all the channels, except one, a Star Trek episode where Bones does brain surgery on Spock while Spock tells him how to do it. He left it there. Billy sat down and they spread out the models on the floor. Billy read his model's instructions.

The first step was a drawing of the inside of the helicopter with the chairs and control sticks and instruments held away from the floor by arrows and dotted lines, like an explosion. The first step read, "Cement seats (38a, 38b) to cockpit platform (4)." Billy searched the trees of molded plastic parts for the seats and the cockpit platform.

Mrs. Calley opened the door. "Nile?" she said, "we're going out for pizza. Get ready."

"Pizza!" said Nile. "Can Billy come?"

"Of course." Mrs. Calley smiled at Billy. "Hi, Billy," she said. "How are you?"

"Fine."

"And how's your mother?"

"Good."

"That's good," she said.

"Can he spend the night?" Nile asked.

"Okay," said Mrs. Calley

After she left Nile whipped his palm out. Billy gave him five.

"Let's start our models," Nile said. He leaned over his kit. Billy glued the seats in place then went to the bathroom. He heard Mrs. Calley yell "You can't HAVE a rabbit" and then a door slammed.

Billy felt sorry for Brian. In the hallway, on the way back to Nile's room, he met Mr. Calley. Billy stepped to the side but Mr. Calley stepped to the same side at the same time. Billy stepped to the other side and Mr. Calley did too. Billy stepped back and Mr. Calley stepped back. Billy stood still and looked at Mr. Calley.

"We dance divinely," Mr. Calley said with a smile.

BILLY AND NILE RODE TO LITTLE CAESAR'S in the back of Mr. Calley's Buick. Mr. and Mrs. Calley sat up front. It was quiet. Brian had run to the basement before they left and wouldn't go with them. Mrs. Calley was mad.

Billy looked out the window. A bunch of custom-painted, jacked-up hotrods in a Seven-Eleven parking lot went by. Some guys were standing around them, smoking cigarettes.

"Nile," Mr. Calley said. "How's about we go visit the Monticello School next week?"

Nile didn't say anything.

"You might like it there," said his mom.

"I bet you would," said his dad. "Lincoln isn't very good. There is a lot to do at Monticello."

"You'd stay there," said his mom. "You could come home on the train whenever you want."

"You don't have to decide," said his dad. "We'll go look at it next weekend, Okay?"

"Okay," Nile said.

Lincoln was the school Billy and Nile went to. It wasn't that bad. The cafeteria sold ice cream, and not many schools did that.

"We think you might like it," Mr. Calley said. "Do you understand? You don't have to. It would be fun and good for you."

"Okay," said Nile. "Let's go."

At Little Caesar's they ordered two deluxe pizzas and two pitchers of Coke. The pizza was good. Billy was hungry and it he devoured it. He and Nile told about riding their bikes downtown and picking out models. They talked about TV shows they liked and what movies they wanted to see.

"I think they show movies at Monticello," said Nile's dad. "They have a planetarium and a swimming pool."

"That would be fun," said his mom.

Mr. Calley said Monticello had a radio station and that the shop class was building an airplane. Billy wondered if he would ever see Nile again after Nile went to Monticello. Nile's parents kept talking about things to do at Monticello, the clothes you wore and what kind of food you got to eat.

After pizza Mr. Calley put the top down and they drove along the river. It was cold out but fun to go fast in the open car. Mr. Calley stopped at Dairy Queen and bought everyone a cone.

They drove to the park and sat on the bank of the river, the sky full of pink clouds. There were ducks in the water and on the bank. One duck was swimming along the flat water with a line of babies behind it. One of them was going in circles with its head hanging down. They threw stones into the water.

"Nile, I have to go to some factories, and we'll be going to France again this summer," Mr. Calley said. "But we're going to have a good time there. That's our mission. We're going to buy a sports car and drive anywhere we want this time."

"What kind of car?" said Nile.

"How about a Porsche," said Mr. Calley.

"Cool!" said Nile.

"We're going to have fun," said Mrs. Calley.

"Brian too?" Nile asked.

"Just us," said Nile's mom. "Brian's going to stay with Aunt Marilyn." Nile's mom had her hand on the back of Billy's neck. She was rubbing his hair. She smiled at him. She had long red hair.

The sun was setting at the park and went down on their way home. The house was solid dark when they got back. Brian was in the basement watching TV when they came inside. Up in Nile's room, Billy sat on the floor in front of his model again. He was tired. Nile put Sneakers on the floor and turned on the TV. *Westworld* was on.

"This is cool," he said. "I've seen this. Let's watch this."

"Yeah," said Billy. He'd seen it too. It had just started. Richard Benjamin and Dick Van Patten were riding to Westworld on a train while a woman described it to them on the PA system.

Nile sat on the floor and they assembled their models while the movie played in the background. Billy worked very carefully at first, looking the parts over and feeling them with his fingertips so he knew exactly what they were supposed to do, testing their fit before he glued them. But after he finished the cockpit, and the engine, he got tired of searching for parts, and he started gluing them as soon as he found them. It went okay for a while, but then some parts didn't fit like the arrows said they were supposed to, and he tried to make them, but they broke, so he left them out. They weren't important anyway. In places the instructions didn't make sense at all. He glued the rotor bezel to the shaft before he inserted the pin retainer, and the blades wouldn't turn, so he had to pry everything part with the glue almost dry. When he put it back together the right way the blades still wouldn't turn and because he had used so much glue and the plastic was soft, they drooped.

"Fuck," he said.

"What's the matter?" Nile said without looking up.

"Nothing," said Billy. "Made a mistake." No loss. He would finish it as best he could, and later, if it was really that bad, he could crash it against the wall or a tree. It would be cool.

His back ached and he looked up. Brian was standing in the doorway looking at him. "What do you want?" Billy said.

"Nothing. Just looking." Brian watched them. Billy put the model in its box, got a gumball out of his pocket, and gave it to him.

Brian unwrapped the gumball and put it in his mouth. "Thanks."

They watched TV.

Richard Benjamin and James Brolin were walking down the street dressed like cowboys. They ran into the character played by Yul Brynner. Yul Brynner was a robot that went crazy.

"Draw," said Yul Brynner.

"Not again," said Richard Benjamin. He thought he had to have another amusement park duel. He didn't know Yul Brynner had a short circuit.

"I'll get it this time," said James Brolin, who thought it was still an amusement park, too.

James Brolin drew his gun and Yul Brynner shot him down. James Brolin looked surprised and said, "I'm shot."

Yul Brynner shot James Brolin dead and said "Draw" to Richard Benjamin. Richard Benjamin said "Oh, god," and took off running through some buildings with Yul Brynner chasing him, shooting.

Billy looked to Brian but Brian had disappeared.

"This is fun," Nile said. He knocked over a bottle of green paint on the carpet and wiped it up with a T-shirt.

Billy went back to work on his model. He felt tired from all that sugar and breathing glue all night. He put the windows and guns and rest of the parts on his helicopter and carried it to the bookshelf. He piled books under the tips of the rotor blades so they would dry straight. He couldn't tell if he had done a good job on his model or not yet because he was too tired. Tomorrow he could hold it and look it over. He knew it wasn't the best model, though. It wasn't such a great kit to start with.

He sat back down on the floor. On TV the movie had ended without him noticing and the news was on. The TV screen floated in front of him. A man named Mr. Backwards was jumping over four school busses in Kansas, on a motorcycle. He was sitting on it backwards, though. He came off over the third bus and landed on his head. It was terrible. Another man, in Texas, had some penguins mixed in with his chickens. He had a refrigerator in the chicken coop with a hole in the door so the penguins could get inside.

Mrs. Calley came in the room and turned off the TV.

"It's time for you to get into bed."

"Okay," said Nile. She closed the door.

Nile put his tank up on a shelf.

Nile had done a good job. There weren't glue smears all over it. The turret turned. Billy knew they would look different in the morning, though. He still had to put the decals on. Sometimes decals helped. They went to the bathroom, where Nile brushed his teeth and Billy rinsed his mouth, then they got in the bunk bed, Nile above, Billy below.

Mrs. Calley came in and kissed Nile goodnight. As she talked to him, Billy looked at her body next to his bunk. She was pretty. Then she sat on his bed and brought her face down to his and kissed him.

She turned out the light.

They were too tired to talk. Billy heard Sneakers bumping around in his box as he lay there, relaxing. His feet were sore.

He woke up in blackness with his heart beating. He didn't know where he was and tried to remember but he couldn't. He was someplace he had never been before. A glowing cube before him slowly became Nile's aquarium. He was at Nile's, in Nile's room. Nile was above him in the bunkbed. Billy lay awake with his eyes shut.

"Billy," Nile whispered.

Billy didn't say anything.

"Billy," Nile said again.

"What," said Billy.

"Let's go down and get cookies."

"No," said Billy.

"Come on," Nile said.

"Okay," said Billy.

They snuck downstairs in their underwear. It was four o'clock. The kitchen was cold. Nile opened the refrigerator and the kitchen filled with light. He took some Oreos from a cookie jar on the counter.

"Here," he said.

"I don't want any," Billy said.

"Go ahead," said Nile.

"No," Billy said. "I don't feel like it. I think I'm going home." He went upstairs for his clothes. Nile followed him. "Wait," he said. "Mr. Jackson has Nazi stuff in his garage. He showed it to me. It isn't locked."

Nile dressed and followed Billy outside. The air was cold in front of Nile's house. Their breaths smoked. The lawns up and down Liberty glistened under the street lights. A car came down the street and Nile ducked into the bushes. "Hide," he said.

He came out after the car went by. "Why didn't you hide?"

"I don't want to," Billy said. He lifted up his bike.

"Yeah you do. C'mon."

"No. I'm going home."

"Don't be afraid."

"I'm not. I just don't want to go to Mr. Jackson's garage."

"You wanted to."

"No, man," said Billy. "I just wanted to make models."

"Chicken," Nile said. He shoved Billy's shoulder.

Billy felt like punching Nile. He had punched Dick Powell in he stomach once and left him lying on the playground after the bell rang. It had made him feel mean.

Billy threw his leg over his bike.

"Baby gets his bottle," Nile said.

Billy rode to his house in the darkness to darkness between streetlights. He wondered where his father was. Just before he got home, he realized with a wave of sadness that his mother was at Clyde's. He didn't even know where Clyde lived. But he could sleep on the couch, and he would hear her when she got home. They would have breakfast together. When Moose, his cat, got hit by a car, they sat at the table and he told her about it. She told him that's the way it was and reached across the table and put her hand on his hand and he felt better. He would wait for her and they would have Sugar Smacks at the table when she got home. He would tell her about Nile and his family. He would tell her about Brian and almost punching Nile, when she got home.

When he got home he found the key under the rock and went inside. He looked at the couch. If he fell asleep on it he might wake up scared and alone. He went to his bedroom and got under the blankets. If she didn't get home before he woke up, he could watch cartoons while he waited. There were some that he liked. If she didn't get home by the time church shows came on, he could leave a note and go bike riding. He would eat some cereal and go to the playground to shoot baskets with the kids that were usually there.

IT'S SATURDAY

THE TAILGATE OF W. BOYD'S TRUCK hung down, scraping. W. Boyd and Hoogstratten had been out in the misty early hours, following the power lines down the bed of Spring Brook, when they got stuck in an eddy of marl. While they were winching it out, cabled to a birch, the truck had lurched, a bale of shingles W. Boyd kept in back for traction sliding into the tailgate, slapping it open with a bang and popping one of its hinges before flopping into the muck. W. Boyd and Hoogstratten were wet and cold now. They were driving to Tabor's house.

W. Boyd could feel the pavement that the tailgate was dragging on through the steering wheel. Hoogstratten shook out cigarettes and they lit them. Then he crouched over and watched the mailboxes come flying by.

W. BOYD LOOKED THE TRUCK OVER in Tabor's driveway while Hoogstratten stood shivering.

W. Boyd liked his truck. It was in good condition and paid off. It had solid aluminum bumpers on it that were supposed to go on International Harvester semi trucks. W. Boyd had mounted them himself. He had bought them at cost from work, an aluminum plant in

Fort Wayne that manufactured semi parts and sailboat railings, bathroom-stall coat hooks, and hundreds of other, different-sized, unidentifiable products, odd shapes packaged in boxes and sent away.

There was no damage, none that W. Boyd could see. He knocked the hingepin out with a jack handle and threw the tailgate in the bed. He wedged a board across the back to keep it in there. The truck squatted in the driveway, dripping mud on the blacktop.

"After we get Tabor let's go to the car wash," W. Boyd said.

Hoogstratten nodded.

MRS. TABOR STOPPED HOOGSTRATTEN and W. Boyd at the breezeway door. Heat from the house poured out. W. Boyd smelled the fresh coffee inside.

"Don't be trackin that mud in here," she said and closed the door. W. Boyd and Hoogstratten sat on cinder blocks outside and loosened the wet laces of their boots and took them off. Mrs. Tabor handed them a blue plastic snow brush. "Sweep each other off," she told them. "Go stand in the grass." They walked out to the lawn in their socks and stood on the hard ground taking turns knocking the mud off each other's pant legs.

The house was warm. They sat at the dinette, forcing Tabor's father, a cabinetmaker at the university, to slide to the back. He was making fishing lures.

Mrs. Tabor set cups of coffee in front of Hoogstratten and W. Boyd and put slices of bread in the toaster. She went to the top of the basement stairs. "John," she hollered, "the boys are here."

Tabor said something from the basement but they couldn't hear what.

"You get out of bed right now," she yelled down.

W. Boyd and Hoogstratten leaned over their coffee. They had their jackets on.

Mrs. Tabor went to the windowsill over the sink and got her cigarettes. She came to the dinette and sat down. She was upset as usual. "Drank his paycheck up again," she said and lit one. She looked out the window.

W. Boyd had met Tabor in third grade. They shared the same, long school bus ride for nine years. They played football together in high school—W. Boyd a lineman, Tabor a receiver, wiry and fast. They'd had their adventures. They hitch-hiked out west after high school and hopped freight trains, riding inside brand new Cadillacs being shipped on rail cars to California, sharing the plush interiors with the local Indians, everybody's feet propped on the dashboard while the hotwired radio played and they smoked marijuana, sagebrush and desert rolling by.

The toast popped up. Mrs. Tabor put the slices on plastic saucers for Hoogstratten and W. Boyd. She pushed a tub of margarine and a jar of cherry jelly across the table.

W. Boyd buttered his toast. "He'll quit."

She turned on him. "He won't keep living here if he doesn't."

Hoogstratten and W. Boyd ate their toast and drank their coffee. When they finished, Mrs. Tabor poured more coffee for everyone. Hoogstratten shook out a cigarette for himself and one for W. Boyd and left the pack on the table.

THEY ALL WATCHED MR. TABOR. He crimped sinkers on fish hooks with a pair of needlenose pliers. He tied tufts of white-tail deer fur to them with dental floss. Then he painted them with yellow enamel. They hung drying in rows along the sides of a shoe box, looking mechanical.

"What you going to do with them all?" W. Boyd asked.

Mr. Tabor took his time thinking about it.

"Give them away," he said.

W. Boyd supposed he meant Christmas. The days were getting shorter and darker and colder.

"What are they for?" Hoogstratten asked. "What do you catch with them?"

"Bass."

"Rainbows?"

"No, rainbows are trout. These here are for lake fishing. Maybe lake trout. But rainbow trout, they're brook trout. You use flies for them. On top of the water."

Hoogstratten nodded. "We just got stuck in the brook," he said.

W. Boyd wished he hadn't said so. "Yeah," he said. "We're going to take John and go wash the truck."

Smoke curled in the light that fell through the picture window, light tinted green by the old glass. Indoors and out, W. Boyd noticed, things looked green. They're used to it by now, he decided, they don't see it anymore. The glass had a hole in it from when he and Tabor were kids in the back yard throwing records in the air and shooting them with a 22.

Mr. Tabor dotted eyes on the lures with a toothpick dipped in red paint. The CB radio and police scanner were going at the same time in the corner of the kitchen.

TABOR CAME UP FROM THE BASEMENT. He was wearing a rumpled cowboy shirt and long johns. His eyes were puffy and red. He came across the kitchen, moving carefully.

They watched him pour coffee. He sat down at the table.

"Wake up, boy," W. Boyd told him.

Tabor sniffed. He knocked a cigarette out of Hoogstratten's pack. His fingers were shaking. He was good with them by now. They were stumps, because two weeks after W. Boyd got him hired at the plant, Tabor lost all eight of them trying to yank an aluminum doorframe out of an eight-ton press. W. Boyd had not been there when Tabor came running out of the pressroom with his hands in the air, but he heard about it later on break.

Tabor held the lighter and sparked it with one hand. He touched the flame, quivering, to the end of his cigarette. He inhaled the smoke and started coughing. He didn't stop for a long time. Mrs. Tabor went to the sink, filled a cherry jelly jar with water, and brought it to him. Tabor sat there breathing with tears in his eyes.

AT THE CARWASH, ALL THE BAYS WERE SHUT. They circled it and found one of the doors raised, so they opened it the rest of the way and drove inside. The stall was dry, but W. Boyd put three quarters in the box on the wall while Tabor held the sprayhead. Nothing came out.

"What a rip," said Tabor. W. Boyd tried to get his quarters back by punching the coin return, but the box wouldn't give them up.

Hoogstratten flicked open his Buck knife. He wanted to cut the sprayhead from its rubber hose.

"No, that's all right," said Tabor. "It's just seventy-five cents." He replaced the sprayhead in its bracket. "Plus we knew it was shut." They got in the cab. W. Boyd backed the truck out of the stall. "Shut that door," he said. Tabor got out and shut the door all the way.

They stopped at Serafino's. W. Boyd bought everybody a sixpack. Then they drove the outskirts, along the strips of fast-food stands, past the mini-storage yards and abandoned gas stations, looking around, scanning the fields, drinking cold Budweisers while the heater blew warm air. Nothing was different, though. There wasn't anything to see, just closed businesses with weeds growing in their parking lots.

Hoogstratten slapped the dash. "Let's go into the woods again."

"All right," W. Boyd said. He leaned forward to look at Tabor. "I'll do that. How about you?" he asked him. "Would you want to do that?"

Tabor was opening a can of beer with his thumb. "Why not."

W. Boyd headed away from town then, out the back roads, past the university, sunlight breaking through the clouds and flickering warm light into the cab, flashing between the trees.

W. Boyd turned into a cornfield, drove through field grass alongside the rows of husks and collapsed stalks to the treeline at the back of the field. They took a two-track through the trees. It led to the abandoned train tracks. They took them deeper into the trees. They knew where they were. The woods were shady and dark.

Hoogstratten thought he spotted a deer, but then he wasn't so sure. "Let's go to the gravel pit," Tabor said. W. Boyd veered off the tracks without slowing down.

Tabor and Hoogstratten leaned forward and held on to the dash, drinking beer as W. Boyd drove wild through the trees, the pickup in four-wheel drive ramming through the undergrowth, flattening saplings, bouncing over rocks, tailgate slamming in back, exhausts hammering.

"Slow down," Tabor yelled, but W. Boyd just turned his hat around and laughed. They came out on a berm near the bottom of the pit. The cliff was as tall as a building, fenced off from the road. The only way to the top was through the woods then up the side of the crater. Gravel spilled down its side.

W. Boyd pointed the truck at the slope.

"Be careful," Tabor said.

W. Boyd tried again and again, getting a running start and curving into the base of the sliding gravel, motor roaring like an airplane, stones spraying from under all four wheels as they climbed, steeper, slower, until each time, they came to a stop and hung there looking into the sky, the truck pressing down, digging in.

Finally they made it to the scrubbier, harder earth near the top, where the tires gathered enough traction to carry them the rest of the way up. The last few feet were near vertical and the truck shot over the lip and came down back wheels first, the front end slapping down so hard the impact knocked the beer from Tabor's hand.

The can foamed on the floor. Tabor picked it up and threw it out the window.

W. Boyd turned the truck around and drove to the edge, where he distributed fresh beer for all, and they lit cigarettes, looking out over the treetops at the city of Fort Wayne. Starlings filled up the branches below them and sang. A flank of Canada geese flew in front of them in the cold opaque sky. W. Boyd could see their feet, black, pressed against their bellies.

He turned up the heater fan, covering the sounds outdoors.

Tabor scooped the bowl of a pipe into a bag of marijuana. He lit the pipe and passed it to Hoogstratten. Hoogstratten toked.

"There's the plant," Hoogstratten said, exhaling just enough to grunt the words out. He pointed to the water tower with the stem of the pipe. They recognized it even though it was just a grey bump on the horizon.

"Hey, man, this is Saturday," Tabor said. He took the pipe out of Hoogstratten's hand and passed it over to W. Boyd.

Hoogstratten exhaled the rest of the way. He looked at Tabor. "What's wrong with seeing the plant?"

"Nothing," said Tabor. "Except you're going to be there for the rest of your life. We ought to give it a breather once in a while."

"Oh, you don't know that," Hoogstratten said. "You may not be there the rest of your life. You don't know what's going to happen to you."

"Do you mind?" said Tabor. "Half the people in that place are lifers. You're going to be working there when you're fifty."

"Drop it," said W. Boyd. He toked, then passed the pipe to Hoogstratten. "If you don't like it, go to college," he grunted. "Be a college professor."

Tabor leaned forward. "I didn't say there was anything wrong with it. I like working with my hands. You're the one who should go to college, Wilson. You like that place too much."

"Ok, so it's Saturday," said W. Boyd. "Let's do something else now."

They chugged their beers and opened new ones. Tabor loaded the pipe again. They passed it. W. Boyd felt himself become stoned. The landscape quilted, the sky turned into a flag. The heater fan hummed and whispered a chord.

A wind buffeted the truck, rocking them in it.

"How about bowling?" said Hoogstratten.

"Right," said Tabor. He waved his finger stumps in Hoogstratten's face.

"Well you can shoot pool and drink beer at a bowling alley, too, you know."

"Let's get out of here," W. Boyd said, shifting into reverse. He backed up thirty feet, then drove forward, accelerating. The truck shot over the edge, nose-diving into the incline and landing in a sideways slide that had him steering furiously to keep from getting caught at right angles to the slope, straightening it out at the last minute.

"Fucking idiot," Tabor said at the bottom.

THEY DROVE THE BACK ROADS, listening to the rock station on the radio and watching the brown trees go by. W. Boyd was hungry. He wanted another beer, but there were no beers left.

They stopped at a culvert to take a leak. Hoogstratten pulled something from the muddy watercress. "Deer skull," he said.

W. Boyd held it by the sockets and washed it, like a part at the plant, poking at the curves and curls in the bone with a clump of pine needles. It was eight inches long, smooth and symmetrical, with exact, sharp, teeth. But it didn't compare with anything the plant made.

"It's a dog," he said.

It seemed to be staring at him, no matter which direction he turned it.

Hoogstratten held it in position while W. Boyd wired it inside the cab to the center of the rear window.

They rode onto the fringes of town, driving through the suburbs with the leaves stuck on their lawns. The sun was getting farther away, turning things dark, heading for the horizon.

"Let's go up on campus and gawk," Hoogstratten said.

"Too cold," said Tabor.

"No one'll be out," said W. Boyd.

He pressed the cigarette pack in his shirt pocket. It was empty. They stopped at the Sportsman's Lounge and bought six cans of Stroh's, take out, and packs of cigarettes from the machine.

Cars started turning on their parking lights as they drove the city streets. Headlights started coming on, making everything around them darker. Shafts of light from the streetlamps bent through the cab as they drove by. Finally it became dark in the cab. W.Boyd pulled the switch that turned on his headlights. The dashboard glowed. He turned down the rheostat, dim, the gauges pale against the blackness.

They rode quietly in the dark cab.

"Let's get some food and take it to Angela's," Tabor said.

Tabor had been working with the women after his accident, running curtain rails through the teflon machine, when Angela's grandmother showed him a picture of her. Angela was studying to be a dental assistant at the community college, her grandmother said. She told Tabor to go to the school and find Angela and say, "Your Grandma Helen told me I should ask you out." Angela was pretty in the picture, and Tabor had done what her grandmother said. He and Angela had hit it off.

Hoogstratten and W. Boyd knew that Tabor would not want to go with them after they'd eaten, but they were hungry and tired of riding. W. Boyd pulled into a Mr. Sam's and they bought a twelve pack and a sackful of groceries for a spaghetti dinner, and they headed to Angela's apartment.

ANGELA WAS WEARING A BIG SHIRT that W. Boyd could see through when she stood in the light. She boiled the spaghetti while Tabor talked to her quietly, standing next to her, stirring the sauce. W. Boyd could see her breasts and the curve of her back beneath the shirt. He wanted to touch her. He wanted to smell her. He wanted to lie in a big, dry bed alongside her body.

W. Boyd and Hoogstratten prepared a salad over the sink. When they finished they went out into the living room and watched football on TV. They drank beer, waiting for the food. W. Boyd was hungry and felt out of place, sitting in the neat apartment in his jacket and boots.

He smelled the food in the kitchen. His mouth watered.

Angela and Tabor brought in plates and silverware and heaping bowls of spaghetti, salad, and garlic bread. W. Boyd couldn't wait to get started. He set his plate on his knees and seared the inside of his mouth on the sauce.

No one talked. They ate quickly, quietly, finishing everything, then sat and watched the ball game come to an end. It wasn't a close game, but there was a kind of excitement in watching the clock run down. When it was over Angela and Tabor went into the kitchen without saying anything and sat at the little dinette and talked.

W. Boyd sat in an armchair in the warm, dark living room with its single lamp in the corner. He looked at Hoogstratten on the couch, awash in the light of the TV screen. He watched Hoogstratten's head bob. Hoogstratten's eyes went white, then closed. He slumped in the corner of the couch, sucking long lungfuls of air through his nose.

Championship Wrestling came on TV. The Iron Sheik chased Hillbilly Curtis around the ring. He grabbed him and threw him to the mat on his head. W. Boyd had once seen a guy get his neck broken that way in a bar.

Looking past the TV, and the walls, W. Boyd felt his face tighten, tingle, then sting. He tasted bitter at the back of his mouth.

He stood up and walked over to Hoogstratten. He swatted him with a pillow.

Hoogstratten's eyes opened without focusing.

"Get up," W. Boyd said.

Hoogstratten leaned forward and stood.

They went to the kitchen to thank Angela and to say good-bye to Tabor. Angela and Tabor looked up, sitting together in the warmth of the dinette.

"It was awful good," said W. Boyd.

Angela smiled.

"See you Monday," Tabor said.

WEAVING DOWN THE ROAD, W. Boyd drove to the plant, day long-since smeared into night. He parked in the supervisor's lot and they looked at the complex. It glittered under the mercury lamps, it vibrated, waiting for Monday morning. W. Boyd smelled aluminum, and his heart raced, the way it raced every weekday morning he lined up to punch in at six-thirty. He rolled his window down. Freezing air filled the cab. He looked out the window at the stars in the sky.

W. Boyd drove inside the yard and pulled up to the storage shed by the loading dock. He got out and took the tailgate and leaned it against the shed. He climbed the incline and stood where the tailgate edge met the wall. He raised his arms to the end of a rafter and pushed with the heels of his hands. The roof, sheet aluminum, creaked up, popping nails, pulling away easy. He pushed until his body was extended, the aluminum roof bowed. He grabbed the top plate and pulled himself up and through the gap, over the wall, dropping down on a stack of billets.

"Boyd," said Hoogstratten from the cab.

W. Boyd was standing on all the billets. They went into the extrusion machine to be heated five hundred degrees then pushed through an extrusion die in the shapes of parts the plant made. They were pure aluminum, a foot long, ten inches around. W. Boyd had always known they were ingots. He used one to knock the hasp off the shed door.

He carried the billet to the truck and set it in the bed.

"What are we doing?" asked Hoogstratten.

"Loading," W. Boyd said. "Load."

Hoogstratten got out of the truck and loaded.

"What are we doing?" asked Hoogstratten when the billet shed was empty, vapor of his breath curling away from him in the cold night air.

The truck sagged, it's suspension bottomed out under the weight. W. Boyd got in the cab. Hoogstratten got in, too.

They drove around the plant, carefully, gently, past the piles of debris, over the scrubby field to the silage pond behind. Processing water from the anodizing tanks cooled in the pond before flowing into the river. It was brown with a cloudy layer of sludge on top.

W. Boyd got out. He took a billet and heaved it like a watermelon into the pond. The water swallowed it with a splash.

"Oh, I see," said Hoogstratten.

They took turns, throwing them in, emptying the truck, one at a time.